"*Succession* meets *The White Lotus* on the open seas."

—Georgina Cross, bestselling author of *One Night*, *Nanny Needed*, and *The Stepdaughter*

"Kaira Rouda has cornered the market on scandal and intrigue among the 1 percent. Suspenseful and glamorous, full of scheming and twists, *Beneath the Surface* is *Succession* meets Elin Hilderbrand."

—Michele Campbell, bestselling author of *It's Always the Husband*

THE WIDOW

"A deliciously diabolical take on marriage, politics, and the lies that bind."

—*Library Journal*

"[A] wild mix of intrigue, secrets, and corruption."

—*Publishers Weekly*

"Rocket-paced, a top-notch political thriller. With hairpin twists and turns, insider knowledge, glamorous settings, and a whole cast of untrustworthy characters."

—Lisa Unger, *New York Times* bestselling author of *Secluded Cabin Sleeps Six*

"Pulls back the curtain to reveal an insider's look at the fascinating and duplicitous world of DC politics."

—Liv Constantine, internationally bestselling
author of *The Last Mrs. Parrish*

"Tense, sharply written, and ticking with suspense, devilishly smart."

—Heather Gudenkauf, *New York Times*
bestselling author of *The Overnight Guest*

"Delicious and darkly comedic tale, pulling back the curtain on the glamorous and backstabbing world of Washington politics."

—Kimberly Belle, internationally bestselling
author of *My Darling Husband*

"Gripping and brimming with insider intrigue, *The Widow* delivers with each scandalous, suspenseful page!"

—Elle Marr, Amazon Charts bestselling
author of *Strangers We Know*

SOMEBODY'S HOME
LISTED IN "BEST THRILLERS COMING IN 2022" BY SHE READS

"Whatever the opposite of family values is, Rouda seems intent on perfecting a genre that enshrines it."

—*Kirkus Reviews*

"Suspense and thriller readers will be on the edge of their seats for this novel that exposes the dark underbelly of human nature."

—*Library Journal*

"There are great characters moving the story along, that sweep away the reader in this story of families, revenge, and secrets."

—*News and Sentinel*

"A truly unputdownable novel that had me gripped—and anxious—from the first sentence! Captivating, fast paced, and unsettling, *Somebody's Home* is astonishingly good. I gulped it down."

—Sally Hepworth, *New York Times* bestselling author of *The Good Sister*

"A gripping psychological thriller you don't want to miss!"

—Lucinda Berry, bestselling author of *The Perfect Child*

"Privilege, social disenchantment, and extreme family tensions are the threads running through this tense novel. Kaira Rouda lets us into the lives of two families and what happens when their paths cross. Gripping and fast paced with an explosive conclusion!"

—Gilly Macmillan, *New York Times* bestselling author

"Taut with foreboding from the first page. An unsettling portrait of an antisocial man, a master of the universe, and the women caught between them. The rotating points of view and incisive, clear writing are sure to keep you flipping the pages until you reach the shocking conclusion!"

—Katherine St. John, author of *The Siren*

THE NEXT WIFE

"Rouda hits the ground running and never stops. So much fun that you'll be sorry to see it end with a final pair of zingers. The guiltiest of guilty pleasures."

—*Kirkus Reviews*

"This gripping psychological thriller offers a refreshing setup. Rouda keeps the reader guessing as the plot takes plenty of twists and turns. Suspense fans will get their money's worth."

—*Publishers Weekly*

"Kaira Rouda knows how to create the perfect diabolical characters that we love to hate. Equally smart and savage, this is a lightning-fast read."

—Mary Kubica, *New York Times* bestselling author of *The Other Mrs.*

"Her narrators are sharp and unpredictable, each one with a tangle of secrets to unravel. *The Next Wife* will leave you tense and gasping, with a chilling twist you won't see coming."

—Julie Clark, *New York Times* bestselling author of *The Last Flight*

"One man. Two wives. Kaira Rouda has masterfully created cunning twists and sharp narration that take you on an unexpected and delicious journey and will leave you with a gasp. Devious and fun."

—Wendy Walker, bestselling author of *Don't Look for Me*

"Nail-biting suspense, dark humor, and family intrigue. I savored every page and now have the worst book hangover."

—Michele Campbell, internationally bestselling author of *The Wife Who Knew Too Much*

"No one writes deliciously devious narcissists like Kaira Rouda. *The Next Wife* showcases her remarkable talent for making unlikable characters alluring."

—Samantha M. Bailey, *USA Today* and #1 national bestselling author of *Woman on the Edge*

"Rouda keeps the pace taut, the action spare, and the characters intense as she takes readers on an hour-by-hour recounting of the couple's fateful getaway."

—*Booklist*

"It's clear from the beginning that something sinister is going on in this novel, which will cost you sleep as you race through its pages. Chilling, satisfying suspense."

—*Good Housekeeping*

"The narrator of *Best Day Ever* is one of the creepiest protagonists I encountered this year."

—*Lit Hub*

"Rich with jealousy and rage, deception and betrayal, a fast-paced page-turner that will keep you on the edge of your seat toward its gripping conclusion."

—*BookReporter.com*

"This book builds like all dark thrillers should, so be prepared for a wallop of an ending."

—*BELLA New York Magazine*

ALSO BY KAIRA ROUDA

WE
WERE
NEVER
FRIENDS

WE
WERE
NEVER
FRIENDS

KAIRA ROUDA

Poisoned Pen
PRESS

Published by Poisoned Pen Press, an imprint of Sourcebooks
1935 Brookdale RD, Naperville, IL 60563-2773
(630) 961-3900
sourcebooks.com

Cataloging-in-Publication Data is on file with the Library of Congress.

Printed and bound in the United States of America.
VP 10 9 8 7 6 5 4 3 2 1

To my Vanderbilt friends.
So happy we are still friends and always were.

"Ever has it been that love knows not its own depth until the hour of separation."

—Kahlil Gibran

PROLOGUE

The pool lies under the velvet cloak of the desert night, its pink and navy tiles glinting faintly in the dim light of the stars. A relic of 1920s Palm Springs decadence, it stretches out in perfect symmetry, its edges softened by the warm hues of stucco walls and the silhouetted palms swaying gently above. The air is still, heavy with the faint, sweet scent of jasmine, and the only sound is the whisper of the breeze threading through the trees.

A mosaic on the bottom of the pool spells out *Desert Sunrise* in elegant, looping letters, distorted by the rippling interplay of underwater lights. The letters shimmer like a mirage, illuminated by the pool lights, their glow a cold, artificial radiance. Suspended below the surface is a figure, a slender form outlined in pale light. Long strands of her hair fan out like seaweed, drifting lazily in the water, a grotesque echo of a mermaid at rest.

Her face is obscured, tilted, but the stillness of her body, the unnatural angle of her limbs, leaves no doubt.

The water is calm, betraying no trace of struggle. It cradles her in its silence, as though the pool itself conspires to keep her secret. Above, the palm fronds whisper their indifferent song, shadows playing along the pink and navy tiles, the grandeur of another era now a backdrop for something chillingly timeless.

As the scene widens, a figure stands at the edge of the tiled deck, shrouded in darkness, outside the reach of the dim light. It's obvious their gaze is fixed on the pool, unmoving, as if mesmerized by the still, spectral presence below the surface. As the breeze quickens and the palm trees sway in concert with some unseen rhythm, the figure melts into the shadows, leaving the pool to its haunted stillness, the words *Desert Sunrise* shimmering mockingly beneath the dead.

MR. AND MRS. RYAN GENTRY

CORDIALLY INVITE YOU TO

A Weekend Engagement Party & Sorority Reunion

CELEBRATING THEIR SON,

Mr. Zachary Gentry

UPON HIS ENGAGEMENT TO

Ms. Celeste Harris

AT OUR DREAM DESERT HOME

PALM SPRINGS, CALIFORNIA

Accommodations and all food and drink provided by your hosts

PLEASE CONFIRM YOUR ATTENDANCE BY

RETURNING THE ENCLOSED RSVP CARD

1

BETH

I'm driving my vintage Mustang, candy-apple-red with a white interior, watching the desert flying by on a gloriously sunny day. I crank up my favorite '80s radio station as "Tainted Love" comes on the radio, and my daughter and I burst into song.

"I can't believe you know this song from my college days," I say, smiling at Celeste, whose feet are up on the dashboard as she pops a red Twizzlers into her mouth.

"Your songs are our songs now," she says. "You know, you look almost the same as you did in college, Mom. I hope I get that lucky."

"Um, thank you," I say, glancing at myself in the rearview mirror. "But I think you need glasses." I see laugh lines next to my eyes and a worry wrinkle between them. My dirty-blond hair is natural, so I guess I'm lucky. I don't have the time, or the inclination, to do anything about the passage of time, which makes me an outlier in Orange County, California. I guess I'm happy with myself and my life. Although I do miss my daughter terribly.

"Want one?" Celeste asks, offering me a Twizzlers from a bag she's pulled out of her purse. Our shared cheat treats.

I grab one of the floppy red licorice sticks and take a bite, grinning at Celeste. I miss her; I miss together time. She's in her second year of law school at Northwestern in Chicago, and it has been hard to let her go, even as I watch her thrive. The curse of a close relationship, I suppose. I take a deep breath and remind myself to enjoy these moments with her, as they are too few and far between these days. My identity for so long was that of a single mom. Now, I'm single, period. Except my cat.

"I hope I left enough cat food out," I say, thinking of Peanut, my fluffy white constant companion.

"You did, Mom; you know you did," Celeste says, her long blond hair glowing in the sunshine. She is effortlessly beautiful. Looking at her makes me think of my best friend in college, Sunny. The resemblance is uncanny, and I smile at the memory and my daughter.

"You're right. Peanut is fine. And I have my next-door neighbor checking on her too," I say, reassuring myself. I think of my cozy bungalow in Huntington Beach and wish I could turn the car around and drive us both back home.

"Mom, I think that's our exit," Celeste says, pointing. She's excited to get there. Me, not so much.

Maybe I was trying to drive past the exit on purpose.

Savoring these last few minutes with Celeste. Alone. We won't have many more moments like this, ever. How did my baby girl grow up so fast?

"Oh, thanks," I say, reluctantly pulling down my turn indicator. I make it over two lanes, and just like that, we're exiting the freeway.

I take another look at my strikingly beautiful daughter, remembering her childhood. It was the two of us while she was growing up, and sometimes it was a struggle, but most of the time, it was happy. We were a team, side by side, like this. But then I remember why we're driving to Palm Springs, and my chest squeezes with sadness. Everything has changed now.

"I still cannot believe you're engaged," I say, shaking my head. "Of course, I'm happy for you. It's only, well, life happens fast." I think that's true for everyone and truer the older you get.

"It does, Mom," Celeste answers, tucking a strand of hair behind her ear. "And then, before you know it, you'll be a grandma."

"Stop," I say. "I'm barely used to this marriage idea. And you have plenty of time. You're only twenty-two." Ever since she told me the engagement news my emotions have been waffling between happiness and panic, but I don't tell her that.

"You were twenty-three when you had me," she reminds me. "You like Zach, and we're in love. Nothing else matters." She takes off her sunglasses, and I can feel her stare. "Right? You're going to be strong and not let anything, or anyone, bother you this weekend. You promised."

I meet her eyes before refocusing on the road. "I said I'd *try*. For you. And Zach. And I will."

The closer we get to their "dream desert home"—leave it to Roxy to wax poetic on a party invitation—the more dread floods my body. My neck is so tense I can barely turn it side to side. It's bad enough being the one my sorority sisters always think of as "the scholarship student." *Poor Beth.* That label sticks for life, no matter how much time passes. But now I'm also the ever-single mother of the bride, who works for a living as president of a nonprofit and barely keeps her head above water with the Southern California prices. I glance at my hands gripping the steering wheel: blue spidery veins and chewed fingernails. I'm sunk before I even arrive. I cannot compete with these women, these so-called friends from college. The fact is I never could.

I snap back to the present as a car almost sideswipes us. As it speeds ahead I note the vanity plate: TINGLEY.

"Jerk," I say under my breath.

"You look pale, Mom. Are you OK?" Celeste asks, touching my leg.

I take a deep breath and force a smile. "I love you. I'm fine. I can handle Roxy for a couple of days. I mean, I handled her for four years in college. I'm excited to make special memories here with you, my favorite girl," I say. "As long as I get to spend time with you, and you're happy, that's all that matters this weekend. Thanks for flying home and driving over with me."

"Of course. How could I pass up one last mother-daughter

road trip?" she says. "Zach wanted to come, too, but his mom insisted he fly straight to the desert. And you know his mom."

"Roxy always gets what she wants," I say. She did back in college, and as far as I know, she still does, every day. It might have been twenty-five years since I'd seen her last, but I have a feeling nothing's changed.

"Yep. That's why Zach and I live in Chicago, far, far away," Celeste says with a laugh. "But not forever. Promise. Just until we finish school, and then we'll be back home. I want to raise all my babies right next to you."

I can't help but laugh with her. Her joy, as ever, is contagious. "How many are we talking now? I know, you hated being an only child, so what's the number up to?"

She grins. "At least four, maybe six."

"And Zach is on board?" I ask.

"Mostly," she says. "He'll come around."

"Ok, bring 'em on. I'm ready," I say. "But not until after the wedding. Deal?"

"Deal, duh," she says. "Oh! It's only four more miles."

She's so excited. I wish the feeling were mutual. "Almost there indeed."

"Come on, Mom. Let me see you smile," she says. "Did you know this is the first time the Gentrys have all come out to the new property? Ryan has been working on fixing it up for two years, I guess. Zach said his dad always wanted a property in the desert, and when this one came on the market, he jumped on it. Didn't even tell Roxy before he bought it."

"Wow, I bet that ruffled Roxy's feathers," I say, stopping at a stop sign. "She never did like surprises."

"Yes, so I've learned. But in this case, from what I know, she wasn't in charge at all. Ryan was," Celeste says. "I think that's the Gentrys' place. On the right."

I still cannot believe my little girl is marrying a Gentry. She'll soon be a Gentry. Of all life's curveballs, this one takes the cake.

"There it is! 26398 Sands Lane. We've made it, Mom," she says, pointing. "Look at that fancy gate and a winding lane beyond."

We made it. Whoopee. Of course Roxy has a big gate to keep out the riffraff, people like me. The gates are magnificent, shiny metal guardians of the property, with a design that is intricate and imposing. Ornate scrollwork and filigree patterns create a sense of luxury and substance. The gate has a decorative crest, GH, displayed prominently in the center. With gates like these, I can only imagine what lies beyond.

I pull into the driveway and stop at the closed metal gates. For a brief moment I have the weirdest sense of déjà vu, like I've been here before. but that's impossible. I've only been to Palm Springs once, ever. I roll down the window and push the call button as hot desert air whooshes into the car.

"It's so warm outside," Celeste says, rolling her window down, too, and sticking her long arm out. "Now it feels like a vacation."

"Hello! Welcome to Gentry House," says a slightly Southern

voice through the call box. Even after all these years, I'd recognize that twang anywhere. Roxy. "Come on in, Beth and Celeste; we've been expecting you all."

I paste on my best Theta Gamma Mu sorority recruitment smile, the one they taught us to use when speaking with an eager rushee who had absolutely no chance of getting a bid on Pref Night. "Thank you," I say through gritted teeth. "Can't wait to see you."

"Mom, relax," Celeste says. "Your shoulders are up in your ears. This is a party for you and your sorority sisters. Roxy has planned everything for a special reunion. I'm excited to meet everyone. It will be fun, not stressful."

"I'm afraid your future mother-in-law has that effect on me," I say. I still cannot believe that fate put these two lovebirds together. That they both picked Chicago for grad school isn't a surprise, as there are a bunch of great institutions there. But of all the young men in Chicago, Celeste had to run into Zach at a party. Ugh.

"You're going to be fine. I'm here," Celeste says. "Ooh, the gates are opening! I cannot wait to see this place. Zach says it's been a money pit but that his dad wanted everything to be restored to its former glory. Apparently, it was originally built in the 1920s as a private compound for a movie star. Can you imagine?"

As I drive down the winding gravel road I notice the mature landscaping. Palm trees and other tropical desert greenery shade our drive as we head toward the house, or rather a cluster of houses that look like typical Palm Springs abodes, with white stucco walls and low-slung tile roofs. It does feel like another era, another time. Sunshine and seclusion, a hideout for the rich and famous.

I once read that in the 1920s, Palm Springs society epitomized opulence and leisure against the stunning backdrop of the California desert. As the allure of the desert oasis grew, the elite flocked to this sun-soaked paradise, transforming it into a glamorous playground for the wealthy. Lavish resorts and exclusive country clubs dotted the landscape, hosting extravagant soirees at which socialites, Hollywood stars, and business magnates mingled beneath the swaying palm trees.

Polo matches, tennis, and golf became popular pastimes, showcasing the leisurely pursuits of the affluent. During Prohibition, speakeasies offered private escapes, adding an air of rebellion to the high-society scene. Palm Springs in the 1920s radiated an aura of indulgence and sophistication, forever etching its name as one of the "it" places when it came to glamorous American history. I suppose it is all of that still. I'm too wound up to appreciate it.

2

ROXY

I stand in the primary suite in front of the floor-to-ceiling windows that overlook the winding driveway and the lush, perfectly manicured grounds. The view is incredible, especially with the palm trees swaying in the breeze. A glass of wine and a good chaise lounge, and I could probably convince myself it's paradise, but there's something about all this space that feels sterile. My guests will arrive soon. It's not going to be pretty, unfortunately. I know my old sorority sisters will feel the same way. This place looks like the goddamn Desert Sunrise. There's no denying it. My husband has spent nearly two years of his life re-creating a nightmare.

I paste on a smile and begin pacing the large room, the soft click of my heels on the polished floor echoing in the vast, renovated space. The walls are a creamy white, the kind that looks expensive, and the furniture is all clean lines and soft textures. But I can't help thinking it's trying a *little* too hard to impress.

On the wall above the sofa, there's a massive Slim Aarons photo, the epitome of mid-century glam. This one's of a pool party in some impossibly fabulous backyard, with bronzed women in bikinis and oversized sunglasses lounging like movie stars, and men in pressed linen shirts holding martinis. It's staged, obviously, but it's the kind of idealized setting that makes you want to crawl inside it and never come out. If you squint, you can almost feel the champagne bubbles tickling your nose.

To the left is the closet. The closet. It's practically the size of my first apartment in Costa Mesa. Rows of designer clothes hang like trophies, every hanger spaced exactly an inch apart, every rack organized by color and season, just like at home in Newport Beach. Shoes are lined up like soldiers, glossy and perfect. And my jewelry that I decided to bring out here sparkles behind the glass cases—bracelets, necklaces, rings. Too much. There's no way I could wear it all, but it's nice to know I could try.

The bathroom might take the cake, though. The soaking tub is so massive it could double as a plunge pool. White marble everywhere, so pristine I feel guilty for even breathing near it. There's a rainfall shower too, of course, with jets that could blast away ten years of stress. I imagine Ryan and me rekindling our romance in this luxurious bath, and it makes me smile.

Ryan and I have been drifting apart, no small thanks to this project taking up all his time. But I'm going to fix everything. After this weekend, and the engagement party, and the wedding, we'll focus on each other. For now, I'll focus on making Zach's marriage one for the ages.

I pause in the middle of the room, taking it all in. It's the kind of place someone like me is supposed to love—beautiful, expensive, excessive. I check out my reflection in the mirror: perfection that has come at a hefty price. But I'm worth it. I've made the Gentry name into one of the most notable in Orange County. I blow myself a kiss and walk back toward the front windows. I can't shake the feeling that something about it all feels off. There are a lot of things wrong in my life, but I'll deal with them after this weekend is over.

Today, I get to see Zach, and that's all that matters. He's my son, my only child, and together with my husband, these two men are my life. I mean, I love to host parties, and I raise so much money for charity in Orange County that I'm a legend. But at the heart of it all, it's my boys I care about. And I'll make this weekend perfect for them, for my boys and for Celeste too.

I hear tires on the gravel driveway as I move back to the windows. A car pulling up. It's an old dumpy something or other that's bright red. Horrible. I take a deep breath as I hurry out of the room to greet them.

Let the games begin.

3

BETH

"Looks like we have a welcoming committee," Celeste says, bringing me back to the moment. I follow her gaze and see that Roxy has appeared. She stands in the middle of the circular drive, next to a gurgling fountain. Roxy Callahan Gentry. She's sleek and refined and clearly as attention-seeking as always—gigantic black sunglasses covering most of her face, blond hair in blown-out beachy waves glowing in the vivid sunshine. The hair color must cost a fortune, and with the thickness, the extensions must weigh pounds. She's wearing a vibrant orange silk dress in a style that is eerily a nod to the flappers of my imagination, low-cut to display her cleavage, as always, and so much jewelry I can't begin to guess what it all adds up to. All in all, she looks like a bright desert Barbie mirage.

Wishful thinking. I blink and she's still there.

I stop the car and Celeste hops out first, running to embrace

Roxy, who resembles an orange slice in the beaming hot sunshine.

"Thank you for having us," Celeste says. "I'm so excited for this weekend!"

"Of course, darling, and you should be excited. I've gone all out, some would say overboard, sparing no expense," Roxy says. She turns her attention to me. "Beth, so good to see you after all these years. Our reunion will be unforgettable, and of course, it's all because of your daughter and my son. True love bringing all of us Theta Gamma sisters together again."

She reluctantly releases my daughter from their extended hug but holds her hands. "Celeste, I know your poor mom would gladly host a celebration like this if she could, but of course not everyone is fortunate enough to have the resources that we do. So, we're happy to step in, for this event, the real engagement party next weekend for which we already have a hundred and fifty RSVPs, the bridal shower, the wedding, rehearsal dinner, all of it. What a joy, don't you agree, Celeste?"

"Absolutely, Mrs. Gentry." My daughter already knows it's best to suck up to Roxy, to agree with whatever she says. We all learned that quickly in college too. I suppose my daughter isn't faking it. Celeste is truly that kind.

"How many times do I have to tell you to stop calling me Mrs. Gentry, darling? I'm Mom now, or I will be soon enough." Roxy steps around Celeste and gives me a less enthusiastic hug. It's limp and, without any body fat to pad her bones, full of angles, like her. "How ironic the young people found each other and brought us all back together," she says in my ear. "I have to say, I've always wondered whether it was strictly a coincidence. Did you know my son was in Chicago? Did you happen to mention it to Celeste?"

"I'm afraid you're giving me too much credit for matchmaking. This was all quite a shock to me too. When Celeste told me you've invited other members of the sorority, well…" I manage to say as we hug. Of course, I never would have guessed it either that my daughter would fall in love with Roxy's son. The strong hair spray holding her perfect blowout in place tickles my nose, and I almost sneeze. "Who got the invite? Celeste didn't know."

"Oh, you'll find out soon enough," Roxy says. "And, yes, much too much time has passed, but now these kids have brought us back together. Love wins," Roxy says. Her fingernails are long, perfectly manicured, and painted the same orange as her dress. One of her diamond-studded bracelets is digging into my back.

I'm so disoriented by the ambush that I missed seeing Ryan, Roxy's husband, appear to greet us.

I break free before I can answer her and wave to Ryan as he walks up. When he smiles, he looks like I remember him in college, although that can't be true. We've all aged as we've raced through life. His blue eyes still sparkle, but his thick brown hair has a dusting of gray at the temple, the only sign of age. I give him a genuine smile and know my dimple is showing. I'm surprised to realize I've missed him.

"Welcome, Celeste! Great to see you, Beth; it's been far too long," Ryan says as he gives each of us a hug. "Let's grab your things and get you both settled." As I pop the trunk with my remote and walk to my car, he follows close behind. "I wasn't sure you'd accept the invitation, truth be told."

"And miss the chance to celebrate my only daughter's engagement? What kind of mom do you think I am?" I say.

"It wasn't the party I thought you might object to. It was, well, the location," he says.

I look at him, his kind eyes, and sigh. "You're right. I won't pretend it's easy to be back here in the desert, but this weekend isn't about me. It's about Celeste and Zach."

Ryan perks up. "That's the spirit. And I really do think you'll love this place once you see what I've done with it. The renovation has been a labor of love, a tribute to the past, so to speak," he says. "Glad you both are here."

I look at his face, about to remind him that I've never been comfortable about visiting the desert again, that I'm only here because of Celeste. But there's something in his eyes—some blend of sorrow and understanding—that makes me turn and look toward Gentry House again. Only glimpses of the rooftop are visible through the thick landscaping. I'm dizzy and stumble into the side of the car. Ryan grabs my hand to steady me. I feel his stare. He's watching me closely. I stare back at the pathway and notice the towering palm trees cast playful shadows over a mosaic-tiled pathway leading to the grand entrance of the house in the distance. And then I know where I am. My mouth drops open.

"Is this the Desert Sunrise?" I ask, dreading his answer. "How? Why would you do this?"

"No, of course not! That old place was torn down years ago. This was built in the same era, so there are similarities, of course," Ryan says. "The architecture of the 1920s is quite specific to the desert, so many of these places look similar, with common amenities and features. I wanted to embrace that era and save one of these grande dames. And I have."

He touches my shoulder as I fight to gain my equilibrium. I haven't stepped foot inside their house, and still the terror has begun. "I don't know if I can stay."

"Don't say that. You've never been here, Beth. Gentry House has been completely refurbished. You'll love it here. I bought this place to save it from being torn down like the Desert Sunrise was and like so many of these homes have been. People don't respect the past anymore, not like I do at least. I couldn't let another demolition happen, not to another one of these historic properties," he says. "It's as simple as that. You're safe here. I promise."

I take my hand away from his and fold my arms across my chest. Nothing is simple, not anymore. Maybe never. I don't feel safe either. I take a deep breath.

"OK, let me think," I say and kick the toe of my tennis shoes into the gravel driveway. I need to calm down. I feel Celeste and Roxy watching me from the other side of the car. I remind myself we are only here because of my daughter. She made the mistake of falling in love with Ryan and Roxy's son. Fate. Ugh.

"Look, Beth, I didn't know Roxy was going to host the engagement party here. I swear. She planned it all and sent the invitations. She's never even been out here until now. I assumed we'd have the party in Newport Beach, at our home," Ryan says. "When I did finally see the invitation, I thought about calling you to warn you that our second home may seem familiar, but I didn't think you'd come if I did. And you need to be here. For Celeste."

My head is spinning. But I'm here, we're here, and I know I must stay. "OK. Fine. For Celeste and Zach, I'll stay," I say. "This weekend is about them, not me."

"Exactly," Ryan says. "The future, not the past. For all of us."

"What's the holdup, you two?" Roxy asks, joining us. "We'll all get heat stroke standing around out here in the middle of the day. We should get inside to the air-conditioning. I have a welcome drink waiting." Roxy strolls off toward the house, fashionable wedges crunching in the gravel.

It's too late to turn around. Celeste has already disappeared, no doubt looking for Zach. I wonder briefly why Zach didn't come out to greet us. And then I see them—Celeste and Zach sharing a hug and kiss in the shade by the pink bougainvillea. Reunited young lovers need their alone time. I get it.

"Come on, Beth," Ryan says as he grabs our bags and slams the trunk closed. "You'll be fine. This is a completely different location. You've never been here before." He smiles and touches my shoulder, but something about the glint in his eye makes me question him. He doesn't seem like the same guy I knew back in college. Something has changed.

"Beth?" he whispers in my ear, sending a chill down my spine. "Celeste and Zach will meet us inside. Let's go."

"OK, I'm coming," I say, stepping away from him. With no real choice in the matter, I follow him down the winding path, wondering what exactly I'm getting into this weekend.

I am not fine, I realize, as goose bumps dot my arms. Despite Ryan's assurances that this is a different place, and I guess it is, the déjà vu is dizzying and disconcerting. I follow him up the walkway to the estate, a meandering pathway adorned with vibrant desert flora toward an ornate wrought iron gate. The gate, intricately designed with art deco motifs, opens to reveal a meticulously landscaped courtyard. We climb a couple of terracotta steps to reach the front door, an artful masterpiece itself, with carved wooden details and stained-glass panels that reflect the hues of the desert sun. A pair of antique lanterns flank the door. The air is scented with the delicate fragrance of the pink bougainvillea, creating an enchanting welcome.

It's all quite lovely. Just like the Desert Sunrise hotel was twenty-five years ago. God, what am I doing here?

Ryan stops and turns around. "It's OK, Beth you'll see. We'll make new, good memories, for Celeste and Zach. I love it here. And you will too."

Ryan is waiting for an answer, his hand on the brass doorknob.

"OK," I say, taking a deep breath. "I'll be fine."

Ryan smiles in relief but then looks over my head, eyes darkening, and says, "We have more company."

4

JAMIE

I look over at Greer, who is driving my white Volvo too fast, and shake my head.

"We really aren't in a rush, honey," I say, still second-guessing the decision to come here at all.

There were so many other things we could have agreed to do this weekend. We could've gone to the medical conference in Miami, where I was invited to speak with an all-expenses-paid mini vacation. I could have spent the time catching up on my research. As a cardiologist, I always have some new medical news to review, new treatments and trials to consider. I'm committed—some, like my husband, would say I'm too committed—to my work, to saving lives.

It's all I've ever wanted to do. Since college, or really since I was a kid growing up in the Valley. I knew what I would become. And here I am. All my dreams have come true. Sort of.

"How much farther?" Greer asks, perfecting his grumpy husband routine. He doesn't want to be here either. I open the app on my phone.

"Looks like about five miles," I say. "Let's try to make the best of this, shall we? Roxy gets on everyone's nerves, not just ours. But I need her in my circle. I need her funding, her fundraisers. And heck, she thinks I'm a…and I quote, *Top Doctor Rock Star*."

Greer laughs. "She does always introduce you that way to big groups."

"Huge rooms full of donors, don't forget. I have a wing at the hospital with my name on it thanks to Roxy," I say.

"You two are the most unlikely friends," Greer says, shaking his bald head. "I mean, she's the blond bombshell life-of-the-party gal, and you're, well, you. Serious, committed, professional."

"We were never friends," I say. "We were sisters. That's what brought us together. Good old Theta Gamma."

"We're here," Greer says, punching a button on a keypad. We watch as the giant gate swings open, and he drives inside. I feel my shoulders tense, as if something is going to jump out of the bushes at us.

I tell myself to calm down. This is a celebration weekend for Zach and Celeste, and for Roxy, Ryan, and Beth. Nothing to worry about. And before I know it, we've arrived.

Ryan stands in the driveway greeting us and hurries to the car, pulling open my door and offering his hand. "So glad you could be here, Top Doctor Rock Star." We hug and air-kiss as Greer climbs out of the Volvo.

"It's a thousand degrees out here," Greer says to Ryan as they shake hands.

"It is," Ryan agrees. "Let's get you inside to the air-conditioning. Everybody else is here."

Greer pops the trunk, and I watch as the two men grab our suitcases. I grab my doctor's kit and my purse.

"I can't believe this is all the luggage you brought. Roxy filled a small moving van," Ryan says.

"Well, she did move in here recently, right?" I say in her defense.

"She arrived a little before you did. I just finished the project, and yes, it's been a labor of love," Ryan says, his eyes gleaming as he leads us down a winding, lusciously landscaped path. What must this cost in upkeep? I wonder as I follow him. We reach a magnificent front door, and a chill runs down my spine. It can't be.

"Ryan, is this…" I begin but he holds his hand up, shaking his head.

"No, that place was demolished. This is my place. Welcome to Gentry House. Let's get inside and cool off." He opens the door, and I'm swept into the home.

I scan the grand living room, the stone fireplace anchoring one wall, the layout familiar and haunting. Of course, this is not the same place, not the hotel of my nightmares, I remind myself. That hotel was miles away from here, I assure myself, and now, according to Ryan, it has been demolished. But still, when I look around, I'm transported back there. I take a deep breath. The furniture and decorations are different, and that's what I try to focus on.

All the furnishings are new and I'm sure very expensive. The framed black-and-white photography from the 1920s is stunning and sets a cool retro tone. I imagine old movie stars, some from the silent picture days, hanging out, enjoying cocktail hour. My shoulders begin to relax. I take a deep breath.

"Nice place you have here, Ryan," Greer says. "Feels like a celebrity should be living here, a Frank Sinatra–type guy."

"Actually, one did live here a long time ago. It was originally built for the actress Gloria Swanson. If only the walls could talk, if you know what I mean. Legend has it that Joe Kennedy slept here. Now it's only us Gentrys," Ryan says. "And the ghosts of the past."

Ryan smiles at me as another chill sweeps down my spine. Must be the air-conditioning, I tell myself.

Roxy walks into the front foyer and squeals. "The rock star has made it!" She rushes to me and gives me a bony squeeze and an air-kiss near each cheek.

"Thank you for inviting us," I say with as much enthusiasm as I can muster. I see Beth behind Roxy. "Hey, Beth! So great to see you!" Even though we live in the same area, Beth and I run in completely different circles. Her nonprofit work, like my practice, takes precedence in her life.

"So happy to see you, Jamie," Beth says, and we share a genuine hug. Compared to Roxy's over-the-top greeting, Beth's feels like home. Like college. Like sisters. I decide I'll try to relax and enjoy this weekend. I wrap my arm around Beth's shoulders.

"Congratulations, mother of the bride. Who would have guessed two Theta Gamma offspring would find each other in Chicago?" I say.

Beth's expression says she's still getting used to the idea too.

Roxy wedges herself in between us, an arm on each of our shoulders. "Isn't it the most romantic, perfect thing ever? My son is a catch, and Celeste is perfect. And now you two are here to share the weekend with us. We're all so blessed, aren't we, Ryan?"

Ryan flashes Roxy a tight smile. "Oh, we are something, that's for sure. And now, the gang is all back together. Let's go have a drink."

It's hard to miss the tension between the Gentrys, but I'm sure weddings are stressful. And bringing us all back together again, in the desert, well, that's bound to stir up memories, good and bad.

Before we can follow Ryan down the hallway, the doorbell rings. Roxy jumps.

"What the heck?" she says as she pulls open the door. "You were not invited here."

5

AMELIA

How could I not show up? I mean, come on. There is no Theta Gamma reunion without yours truly, and they all know it. Someone…ahem, Roxy…forgot to send the invitation to me, I'm sure of it. Besides, with all the mourning, or pretend mourning, I've been doing over my recently deceased husband, maybe I missed it. So many condolence cards were clogging our Georgetown mailbox it was obscene.

Yes, he was a long-serving senator with huge power. And because I was Senator Dell's wife, I had a lot of power on the Hill myself. I know as much as anyone, you're only as powerful as your elected spouse up there in DC. So, my time is coming to an end there. It's time to reintroduce myself to Orange County, California. With all of the money my husband has left me, I'll return in a surge of financial freedom and live the life I was meant to live.

I've always had money, I remind myself as I stand outside this lovely mid-century compound. My family was on the *Mayflower*. If you say the last name Alden, most people in the Northeast will recognize it. My ancestor was John Alden, a prominent figure in the Plymouth Colony. And up to my daddy, the Aldens prospered and thrived.

My grandmother's pearls around my neck are starting to feel moist. Ugh, I'm sweating, it seems. I run my hand behind my neck and lift my red hair. I can't stand here any longer; I need to ring the bell. I came here on a lark, and really, I have nothing to lose. I don't need any of these people. I have more money now than I can ever spend.

No, I don't *need* them for anything. But this is going to be fun. Ever since I saw Celeste announce a special Theta Gamma reunion out in the desert, I knew I'd be here, one way or another. Celeste is such a lovely ray of sunshine. She reminds me a lot of Sunny. Always smiling, always upbeat. At least that's what Celeste looks like on her social media. We'll see if she's the same in person.

I grab the big iron door knocker and let it drop before pushing the doorbell. I'm entering with a bang, some might say. I can't wait to see Roxy's face when she sees me. She won't have an expression, of course, because she's had too much work done. Mine is subtle, East Coast light touches. Roxy is over the top, and I love sticking it to her, always have.

6

BETH

I turn to look out the front door past Roxy and spot Amelia Dell, looking as glamorous as she was in college, and, I'm sure, as rich with her family's generational money and her newly deceased husband's estate. She was a legend back in the day, with the highest weekly allowance of any of the sorority sisters. And with her red hair, still long and styled in waves, her classic designer wardrobe, porcelain skin, and her willowy height, she demands attention wherever she goes. Now that she's a widow, with all her husband's money to spend since his untimely death from a heart attack, she has more power than ever.

"Hey, Amelia," I say with my rush smile. "I'm so sorry about your husband. But it is good to see you."

She laughs and gives me air-kisses near both cheeks. "Well, yes, it was a shock when he died like that, but he had become rather bothersome, to be honest. So, well, that settled itself. I guess you've been there, Beth, with that husband of yours dying so young. Maybe that was a blessing after all. It's good to see you. Ryan, you're looking as handsome as ever, you devil. You don't age. What's your secret?"

Ryan flushes with the overt flirting. "Good to see you, too, Amelia."

"Look at the all-important doctor. Come over here for a hug," Amelia says. Jamie grins and they share a hug.

"You remember my husband, Greer," Jamie says as Amelia and Greer shake hands. It's clear Amelia doesn't remember Greer, not at all.

Roxy's hands are on her pointy hips. "Amelia, *you* were not invited here."

Oh my God. Amelia is crashing the party. Unbelievable. I cover my mouth with my hand so no one can see my smile.

"Oh, Roxy, don't be silly. I'm sure my invitation got lost in the mail," Amelia says, wrapping Roxy in a hug. "That's better, sister of mine. Theta Gamma for life."

Roxy's speechless for a moment as she steps away from Amelia.

"I'm assuming a plus-one is OK with you too," Amelia says, pointing behind her. He's coming along right behind me. "Since my invite was lost, I presumed it was OK."

Roxy shakes her head. "You really are something."

And then I see him, a guy farther down the path, struggling to manage her three large pieces of Louis Vuitton luggage. I look at my beat-up carry-on suitcase against the wall in the foyer and shake my head. I'm so out of my league.

As he comes closer, I realize her luggage valet and date looks vaguely familiar. Or maybe my déjà vu about the house is coloring everything I'm seeing now.

"Well, here he is. You two remember Brett Logan?" Amelia says after air-kissing her now sweating date. "We ran into each other at a bar not long after my husband died, and he's been such a comfort to me. Life has been a whirlwind, as you all can imagine. I have the kids to worry about. Their grief over their dad, and my own, of course. It's all so complicated. But as I always tell the kids, nothing that comes easily is worth having."

Ryan and I nod along with Amelia's life story, while I watch Brett. He's definitely familiar, but I can't place him.

"Anyway," Amelia says, finally taking a breath and seeing us again, "since this is a mini-college reunion, I thought, why not bring a fellow Southern California University grad? Brett, do you remember Roxy, Beth, Jamie, and Ryan?"

Roxy doesn't make a move to welcome this additional guest. And if looks could kill, well…

Seemingly unfazed by the icy reception, Brett manages to set all of Amelia's luggage down before extending his hand. It's damp with sweat.

"Nice to see you again," he says to me. He puffs out his chest and seems to flex his well-defined biceps. He must have been a college athlete. I'd guess football. His hair is cropped short, with a touch of salt and pepper. He exudes jock vibes, someone who has maintained his physical prowess and is proud of it.

"Were you in our class?" I ask. Brett looks smug, in that way in which a guy who has always been handsome is. Like he's above us all.

"I was a little before your time. Not much. I was on the SCU football team, the squad that won the championship."

"Nice," Ryan says. Because what else do you say to an achievement decades old? Someone's clearly still trying to relive his glory days.

Amelia swoops in, sliding her arm through his, making her claim. "Anyway, Brett was my TA way back in the day, when I took a prerequisite science class. We reacquainted ourselves at a bar in DC when he was in for a meeting," Amelia says. "It's sort of like dating the professor." She winks. "Which, of course, I also did in college."

"Of course," Ryan says, laughing. "Welcome to Gentry House, my pride and joy. We have plenty of room. Let's get some beverages and cool off."

Roxy exhales.

Ryan says, "You have to let them stay now, don't you? I mean, I know you like to control everything, but why not go with it? You used to be spontaneous, when you were young."

I swallow, waiting for Roxy's reaction as I take in the baby grand piano, the centerpiece of the living room and foyer area. A Steinway, of course.

"Fine, Amelia, you win," Roxy says.

"That's the spirit, sis," Amelia says with a grin.

"Let's go have that drink, shall we?" Ryan says, leading the way.

The tension in the air is suffocating as we all follow Ryan. And then there's the past that's haunting me too. We arrive in the kitchen as Roxy has regained her composure and takes charge of the room. She smiles at all of us, but her eyes have gone chilly.

And for the second time today I'm reminded that Roxy hates surprises.

7

BETH

I have to hand it to Amelia. Only she could find the nerve to crash a party. I'm surprised she wasn't invited originally, since she was a big part of our group in college. She's definitely on Roxy's last nerve now. Maybe it comes from being Roxy's closest confidante back in college; she knows what buttons to push.

As we walk down the hallway, Brett extends an olive branch to Roxy. "I'm sorry for being here. I thought we were invited."

"You weren't," Roxy says but pastes on her sorority rush smile. "And you two met at a bar?"

"We did, yes," he says.

"Apropos," Roxy says with a smirk.

"Brett will be a good boy, Roxy. And I'll be a good girl. Come on, lighten up," Amelia says as she knocks her bony elbow into Roxy's equally bony side. Amelia's pearl necklace is a stark contrast to Roxy's flashy diamonds. But equally impressive. "The more the merrier, right?"

Roxy's blue eyes flash, but a smile returns to her face as she tosses her blond hair over her shoulder. "Sure, fine. We'll put you two in the pool house. It's a big space and out of my way," she says.

"Ooh, fun; we like our privacy," Amelia says and winks at Brett.

Ridiculous.

"But first, our welcome drinks," Roxy says. "I'm sure you're parched, Amelia. I only hope my cocktail-making skills live up to what you're used to on the DC social circuit. It seems like every time I see your photos online, there you are with a drink in your hand. All that glad-handing on the Hill must be thirsty work."

"Ha, yes, my husband's communications director mentioned that I was a regular in the society pages on the Hill and back at home in Orange County. We were a power couple. I'm afraid I've been too busy to look at them myself, but I'm sure I'm the media darling du jour because of Dick's sudden death. The widow sympathy, I suppose. Sooner or later they'll point their cameras in another direction," Amelia says through tight lips.

I'm glad she didn't add that the press likes her better than Roxy. I know she wanted to. *This is going well*, I think, feeling the familiar tension of one-upmanship fill the room. These two are born sparring partners, have been since college. The term "frenemy" springs to mind. I have no idea if Amelia still enjoys drinking as much as she did back in the day, but in our undergrad years, she was rather notorious. I don't read the society columns, for obvious reasons, nor have I ever been photographed for the party pages. Roxy and Amelia both appear regularly in their respective cities, I'm sure.

Roxy and Ryan lead us into a thoroughly remodeled and modernized kitchen, nothing like the one in my college memories, thank goodness. The original terra-cotta tiles have been meticulously restored, and the cabinets, no doubt inspired by Spanish Colonial design, are rich dark wood, with carved details and wrought iron hardware. The warm color palette is a nod to an earlier era, with earthy tones like terra-cotta, muted blues, and olive greens. Sunlight floods in through the windows, accentuating the gleaming stainless-steel appliances and the polished granite countertops. The backsplash features what must be hand-painted tiles in vibrant colors and geometric patterns. Open shelving displays a curated collection of vintage cookware, adding even more character to the space. I'm captivated by the charm of the kitchen and decide that maybe everything will be fine.

"Hey, wait a minute," Amelia says. "This place feels familiar."

My shoulders find my ears again as my neck tenses. Ryan touches my shoulder.

"I'm certain you've never been here, Amelia. It was a family estate until we bought it," Ryan says. "I know your husband did a lot of fundraisers out here in the desert, so maybe it reminds you of one you attended."

"No, it's not a place I've been for a fundraiser. I know, it feels like—oh my God, that place we stayed during senior year, that horrible trip," Amelia says. Her face has drained of color, and as she leans back against the kitchen counter, her black linen dress seems to crumple with her. "Now I do need that drink."

"And we'll be happy to oblige you. But I'm surprised you remember much about that trip. You hit the margaritas pretty hard, if memory serves," Roxy says airily.

"It was spring break. Margaritas were practically a requirement. And I was hardly the only one in the bar," Amelia says with a huff, her New England accent coming through when she is angry like it did in college. Brett chuckles beside her until she narrows her eyes at him.

"Well, in any event, Gentry House might share some design elements with where we stayed," Roxy says, "but this place has never been a hotel, always a private residence. Ryan bought it for me, to save it from being torn down. It was such a lovely surprise. He's so thoughtful," she says, placing her diamond-encrusted right hand over her heart. "So romantic, too, don't you think? I mean buying this whole place and fixing it up, all for me."

"Whatever floats your boat, I guess," Amelia says. "It's a little creepy how much it looks like that spring break hotel. Much nicer decor, but the same feeling in every room I've seen so far. I mean the entry foyer was like the hotel's; this kitchen is nicely redone, but the bones are the same. You do see that, don't you? But glad you're happy with the surprise," Amelia says, shaking her head, clearly as stunned as I am with their choice of a second home.

Ryan walks over to what must be a vintage wooden tray bearing a dozen or so orange-colored, fizzy-looking cocktails in festive crystal glasses. Each drink is adorned with an orange slice and a white-and-orange-striped straw.

Ryan hands one to me. "Aperol spritz, Roxy's favorite. Of course."

Of course. Whatever Roxy wants, Roxy gets. I accept the cocktail with a smile.

"Cheers, Beth!" Ryan says before turning to fetch some more Aperol Spritzes.

"Cheers," I say as Zach, who looks just like his dad, and Celeste burst into the room, holding hands, blissfully unaware of the tension of the moment. They only have eyes for each other. It has been a whirlwind courtship. When Zach popped the question, I was been shocked.

"Are you sure about this? It's so soon," I'd said to Celeste when she called me with the good news.

"Mom, when you find Mr. Right, you know it," she'd answered. She turned on FaceTime and showed me the huge diamond engagement ring. "Isn't it gorgeous?"

I had to admit it was, but why the rush? "It is. And you are too. But you're in law school and, well, you're young, honey."

"Mom, why can't you be happy for me?" she'd said, her face falling into a frown.

I'd taken a deep breath. I should be happy for her; I knew that. Fate works in mysterious ways. I smile at Celeste now, so happy, sipping an Aperol Spritz, Zach's arm wrapped around her shoulders.

"What a reunion," Brett says as he grabs a drink from Ryan and slaps him on the back. "Who would have thought I'd be here with all of you popular people. It's great."

He continues to annoy me, but I'm not sure why. I guess it's the good-old-boy, jock act. He's too old for it.

"If you were hoping for a college reunion, I'm afraid you've come to the wrong place. This is a celebration for my daughter and the Gentrys' son," I say to Brett as I feel a headache brewing behind my eyes. I need to lighten up, I know I do. "We are all here for them. This is their weekend." I press my fingers against my temple hoping to dull the pain.

Celeste is by my side, welcome drink in her hand. "What's wrong, Mom? Are you OK?"

No. "Yes, I'm fine. I want to make sure the guests of honor don't get overshadowed by silly sorority talk. Cheers to young love!"

Ryan meets my eyes and mouths *sorry*. I shrug. What else can I do? I'll need to get over the shock of the setting. I knew I was coming back to the desert, but I didn't realize how triggering Gentry House would be, how similar it would feel to the place I never wanted to see again.

Celeste squeezes my hand. I smile at my daughter. My only choice is to focus on her happiness, on her future, accept the things I cannot change, and try to forget about the past.

8

ROXY

I must admit it has been fun to watch my sorority sisters' startled expressions as they stepped into our vacation home. Ryan's masterpiece. His gift to me, I told them. Aren't I lucky, I gloated.

As if any of that were true.

I felt the same haunted chills yesterday, when I walked through this place for the first time. I hadn't expected to find this at all. I knew Ryan had invested a fortune fixing up our second home, and I trusted, since he'd used my decorator and contractor, that I would love what I saw when I arrived. And he'd made me promise I wouldn't set foot on the site until it was completed. I felt confident sending out the invitations without ever seeing this place.

I learned the truth when I arrived. That's when I realized that Ryan's remodel had created a vacation home for us that looks stunningly like the Desert Sunrise, that godforsaken hotel that haunts all our memories. I'd looked at my husband, who had nothing but excitement and pride in his creation, with wide, mistrusting eyes. He frowned.

"What?" he'd asked, brow wrinkled. "It's perfect. Don't complain. For once, please, let me be happy. It's my place. End of story. You're the one who insisted on hosting this engagement party weekend here instead of at home in Newport Beach. If you're uncomfortable, it's your own fault. Not mine. I'm happy here."

"You *know* what," I'd said, crossing my arms. But I hadn't said anything else. It was a fait accompli. It was ours, for better or for worse. And besides, this little project in the desert had kept Ryan content, much more so than he'd been for years. I told myself I could handle a weekend here now and then. I tried to tell myself the visceral reaction would fade over time, and all I would feel is the care Ryan put into restoring this home. I'd pretend it was his gift to me. I should be grateful, not haunted. This place, I decided, would bring us closer together again.

And now, as I touch up my makeup in the lavish primary suite bath, I'm resolved to relax and enjoy the weekend. This project makes perfect sense for him. Ryan always had an architectural preservation streak in him, and he was looking for a vacation home. This opportunity presented itself, and he jumped at it. That's really all there is to it, so we all need to move on, should have years ago. I hear voices downstairs, touring the house with their welcome cocktails, no doubt. It's showtime. One last time.

I think about them all. Greer and Jamie. They drive a Volvo, of course. Sensible, safe, predictable, and boring. That's Jamie. She still wears her hair in the same blond bob she had in college. Speaking of boring, Greer is still nice enough looking, I suppose, although a little pudgy around the middle and completely bald, poor man. He's always been overly nice, and boring too. They are perfectly middle-aged, almost content with it, and that sort of grosses me out. They're turning soft and a bit wrinkly. They'd be perfect cast as satisfied customers in an ad for a fast-food burger chain. I will fight aging and plumpness with all I've got.

Amelia is still Amelia, and her date is ridiculous. Beth is dependable and malleable. She is, to her credit, the mother of an amazing daughter. I can't wait until Celeste is a Gentry. I knew someday my son would choose a wife, and I've dreaded that day. But he picked her, and she is sunshine, truly. Like our beloved Sunny. She doesn't seem interested in competing with me for anything, and she's comfortable in her skin. I like that in a daughter-in-law-to-be. I really do.

I walk out of the suite and back downstairs, joining the group in the formal living room.

"It reminds me of that hotel we stayed in," Jamie says. "So much. This gravel driveway, the sound of the crunch of the tires. And that entry. Oh my gosh." She clutches her drink in both hands. I notice that she's wearing athleisure black sweatpants and a black T-shirt. She knows better.

"What, the Desert Sunrise? Funny, you're not the first person to mention that today. There are some architectural similarities, I suppose, but that's to be expected from '20s-era buildings." I am smiling as wide as I can as I go into my spiel about the house's movie-star former owner and Ryan's dedication to historical preservation. *See, Jamie, it's fine. Fine with me, fine with you. Get over yourself.*

Jamie looks at Greer, and he shrugs. He doesn't care. He wasn't there. After a moment, she nods as if in acceptance. But her fingers haven't relaxed their grip on her drink.

"Poor Ryan was making the two-hour drive back and forth two or three times a week to oversee all the renovations to this place," I say. I decide to keep talking so Jamie stays distracted. I slip my arm through hers, like we're best friends. "I finally convinced him that it'd be easier if he stayed on-site until the work was completed. He hated being without me, but all that commuting didn't make sense. Now it's done, thank goodness. The only thing we haven't had a chance to upgrade yet is the pool."

I see Jamie's eyes wander past the refurbished stone fireplace, past the baby grand piano, and out to the pool beyond. She walks across the room and pushes a curtain aside to stare out at the backyard, I assume trying to catch a glimpse of the pool. She won't be able to see much from there through the lush landscaping. I push away a chill and rub my arms. I guess I must admit it is eerily like the pool from spring break, but it was the style back then. All the finest hotels and private residences had a tiled pool. It was a status symbol, plus it's hot in the desert most of the time. But it's not the same pool. Period. I hope I've made that clear.

"Thanks again for hosting us," Greer says, leading Jamie by

the hand. He's still excited to be here. I appreciate that in a hamburger chain spokesperson.

"It's my pleasure, of course. It's going to be a perfect weekend, celebrating young love, new beginnings, and all of that."

Jamie meets my eye. "Sure, OK, whatever you say. We're here now."

"This is going to be a lovely weekend. It will be a weekend to remember. I've planned everything, for months, and it was a lot of work. You could be a little more excited about it all," I say. I might have a little more fire in my voice than I mean to, but I want her to realize how hard I've worked to make this weekend a success.

A little Theta Gamma Mu spirit would be nice to see. From all of them.

9

ROXY

I stare at Jamie as she puts on her best Theta Gamma Mu smile. I mean I know she's got it in her. After all, she was my little sister and followed in my regal footsteps, becoming president of the chapter once I graduated. She knows how to fake it.

"You're right, of course," Jamie says, dropping her eyes to the original Spanish tile floor, no doubt admiring its sheen. "I apologize. It's just, well, it, this place, has thrown me off. I can't wait to meet Zach and Celeste."

"That's the spirit," I say, relaxing a bit. Everything is perfect. Everything will be perfect. It must be. Zach is my only child. He picked Celeste, for some strange reason, and I've come to terms with his choice.

Besides, despite the rather unnerving but elegant setting, this is my chance to shine. I want all the attention focused on me. I especially want Ryan to see me in command, and crushing it, with beauty and poise. And I will, of course. Despite being way out here in the desert, everyone who is anyone will hear about this lavish weekend back home at the beach. And then I'll one-up myself with the official engagement party. I can't wait.

They'll all wonder how I pulled it all together, every last detail of this special weekend, knowing there are more parties, more celebrations, on a much grander scale to come for my son and his wife-to-be. I've already tipped off the party and society pages of the magazines, and they're waiting for photos. And I'll supply them, making sure I look the best. I'm excited for what's to come too. There will be over-the-top bridal showers, and a rehearsal dinner so grand it will take every guest's breath away. Yes, the rehearsal dinner should be Beth's to plan, but I'm glad she cannot afford what I want to do. It's all mine.

Do I already have an outfit for each occasion, each celebration? Of course. For example, notice the bright orange Gucci dress I'm wearing now to welcome them, selected to match the Aperol spritz I hold in my hand. This entire weekend will be my own private fashion show, for this deliciously jealous group of sisters.

They say the mother of the groom should wear beige and be quiet throughout the wedding process. That color and that attitude do not suit me. In this case, the mother of the bride will fade into the background. Beth always has been in the background, even though she actually is more attractive than she thinks she is, with her natural dirty-blond hair and big brown eyes. She has an innocent look that turned a lot of heads in college; she just didn't notice them turning toward her. I, for one, was not about to enlighten her and add to the already fierce competition back then.

I lead the boring ones and the rest of the party back into my gleaming new kitchen.

"Attention, everyone," I say in my fabulous hostess voice, "we're all here. Some of us unexpectedly. But it's fine. The more the merrier. Let the party begin!"

I catch a look from my spoiled-rotten son, Zach, whom I love dearly. Oh, of course he's pouting. He wants me to put the spotlight on him too. He has a few of his mom's tendencies, I'll admit, but mostly he's just like his father. I wink at Zach.

"And cheers to Zach and his beautiful fiancée, Celeste, the reason we're all gathered here this weekend," I say.

Zach smiles at me. "Thanks, Mom. This place is amazing, Dad. We're so excited to get this weekend started. Cheers!" He clinks his glass on Celeste's and grins. He has his father's smile, small teeth, poor boy. I glance at my husband. For some reason Ryan isn't smiling, not at all.

I hurry over to his side. "What is it? What's wrong?"

"Nothing is wrong," he says. "Let's show them all to their rooms. I could use a break. You know I didn't want them here but agreed to go along with it, for you. And for Sunny, I mean the memories, you know. And now they're here, and it will be fine. It's overwhelming. I need a break."

"Memories are great, but these are our long-lost friends, our college buddies," I say. "You should be happy to reconnect.

Come on. Cheer up. All your hard work on this house, and now you have a captive audience eager to explore every room. You need to stick around, take us on a tour."

From the look on his face, I can tell he's not buying what I'm selling. And that, despite his assurances, something is wrong with him. He's off.

"I have a call to make, so why don't you show your guests around?" he says before walking out of the kitchen. So rude. I see a few of the guests watching his departure. I paste on a smile. He's acting like a baby. I mean, we're all here now. The weekend has started. What could possibly be more important than getting our guests settled in? Fortunately, before they all arrived, we reviewed which room to put each guest in, so I can settle them in myself. Amelia is a surprise, but that's what the pool house is for. To house people you don't want under your own roof. Ha. She will not steal my thunder or ruin my event. That's not going to happen.

I focus my attention back on Zach, my glorious son. His frown matches his father's. He must have seen Ryan leave. So much for my perfect weekend.

10

BETH

As I expected, my room is elegant, with mid-century modern furniture in white and tan, and, hanging over the fireplace, framed black-and-white photos of a group of people lounging around a pool in the 1930s. The plaque on the wall reads *Famous actress Miss Gloria Swanson and friends enjoying an afternoon at her mansion in Palm Springs.* I try not to look at the pool for too long. Its shape is all too familiar. Out the window, I see the same pool in real life, glimmering in the sunshine.

I walk over and sit down on the huge California king bed, leaning back into the thick, white duvet. I wonder if they had anything terrible happen here or if it was all a fun hideaway for the Hollywood set. Now, it's a fun hideaway for Roxy and Ryan, a place where Roxy can strut her stuff, quite literally, and have all of us around to admire her: her home, her things, her life. Just like back in the college days.

My roommate and best friend always had a way of putting Roxy and other girls like her in their place, though. I remember the day we met, during sorority rush our first few days on campus at SCU. I was hurrying out of a rush party in shame and almost ran into my roommate, who was smiling confidently, climbing the steps to the house.

"Hey, what's wrong?" she asked, tossing her long blond hair over her shoulder. She was stunning, with bright emerald-green eyes that seemed to know everything was going to be all right.

"I don't belong here, doing this," I'd said to my new roommate, holding back tears. I bit my lip.

"Come with me," she said, taking my hand and pulling me out of the incoming sorority recruitment foot traffic and around the side of the Theta Gamma Mu sorority house. "OK, now I don't like this attitude from you. We went over this last night in our room. Just because you're here on a scholarship doesn't mean you don't deserve to be in a sorority. This one, in fact, because it's the best, and this is where I'll be."

I shook my head and wiped the tears from under my eyes. "But you should see, there are some mean girls inside that party. This one, Roxy, she's a freshman, too, but she acts like she's already a member. The look she gave me was…well, she made me feel awful. Like she was judging my outfit, my hair, my everything."

"Oh, I've heard about Roxy Callahan," she said. "She's a top rushee, for sure. But the thing is, even though Roxy is a legacy, and she will likely be chapter president someday, she's harmless.

All that bluster, those looks she's giving, you, it's because she's insecure. That's all. Happy people don't do that; only weak people do."

"She didn't strike me as weak," I said, a smile coming to my face despite myself. "She looked quite powerful, the center of attention. Her blond hair perfectly blown out. And the jewelry? Wow."

"It's all an illusion," Sunny said with confidence. "But we do need to create our own unique selling propositions. OK? I'm the cute girl from San Francisco who has a lot of recs and a certain mystique about who my parents are. Am I of *the* San Francisco Spencers? No, not really. They are cousins. But it gives me a little sparkle, you see?"

I nodded. "Sure. I'm Beth Harrison, scholarship student from Santa Clarita. That's not sparkly at all," I said.

"Wrong!" she said with a grin. "You are Mensa-level smart, and you were from a wealthy family, but when your parents divorced, your dad left with all the family money. He could reappear any minute and you'd be rich."

"My parents *are* divorced," I said.

"Perfect. Stories with a little truth add good sparkle power," she said. "Let me handle spreading the Mensa and money rumor. That should quiet the Roxys of the world. Besides, if they want me as a Theta Gamma Mu pledge, they will take you too. We're a package."

"But we just met," I said. "Why are you being so nice?"

"Because I like you, you're my roommate, and I don't like

Roxy either," she said. "Now let's get inside. I can't wait to see Roxy's face when we walk in together, and when I tell her you're a brain and you're my best friend."

And she'd done that. She forced me back inside the party, held my hand as we marched right up to Roxy, and broke the news that we were BFFs.

"Well, that doesn't make much sense, but fine," Roxy said, her face a little flushed.

"It makes perfect sense, Roxy," Sunny said. "And soon, we're all going to be sisters. Isn't that great!"

I'd never felt more protected, more loved.

Begrudgingly I stand up, walk into my en suite bathroom and look at myself in the mirror. I've pulled myself together as best I could. I'm wearing more makeup than I ever do at home, and my new navy-blue dress, purchased for the occasion, feels sleek and a little chic. I have struggled into some Spanx even, to smooth my curves, and my mousy blond hair is as styled as it can get. I smile at myself, revealing my dimple, my only cute quality. It's true. Everything else, all my shine, has faded away over the years. I'm like an old washcloth you keep around because it's familiar. Or because your son is marrying my daughter.

"It's as good as it's going to get," I say to the mirror. And then, because the only person I can say this to is my own reflection, I add, "I hope Celeste knows what she's doing."

I love my daughter, my beautiful blond daughter, who looks everything like her playboy father. Luckily, she got my brains and personality. The best of both worlds, I suppose. When he died of an overdose when Celeste was a toddler, I have to say I was relieved. I welcomed being a single mom, and I hoped I would do a good job. I can now replace my primary worry of her childhood with my new worry of her adulthood: Celeste is marrying my nemesis's son. And they've only known each other for four months. There's no two ways to look at it. My least favorite sorority sister is now going to be my daughter's mother-in-law.

When Celeste broke the news a few months ago, I was shocked. I knew she and Zach had been dating and then moved in together in Chicago, but a proposal? It was all moving too fast, but there was nothing I could do to change her mind. I suggested waiting until after law school, at least, but to no avail.

I tried to focus on the positive. My daughter will be incredibly wealthy, and well taken care of. Zach seemed to be a wonderful, if not a bit pretentious and entitled, young man. And though I hadn't seen Roxy or Ryan since college, I had to try to believe that Roxy had changed.

But Roxy hasn't changed. It's clear that she's still the self-centered snob she was back then, and maybe worse. There's no kindness, no empathy in her bones, never has been, only an intense striving to be the best, the prettiest, the most popular. Maybe Zach has Ryan's personality; maybe that's what Celeste sees in him. I always liked Ryan, even if I hadn't let myself remember that until today.

I check my watch. I can't avoid dinner any longer. I walk out of my charming and cozy room—I must admit the accommodations are five-star—and make my way down the hall, following the sounds of laughter and chatter floating up from the first floor. I stop and admire a framed black-and-white photograph of a woman in a bikini standing by a pool. She's facing the pool, her back to the camera, her long blond hair halfway down her back. I swallow as the memory of Sunny's long blond hair pops into my mind. Plenty of young women have long hair, I remind myself, as I hurry down the stairs.

I hear a voice coming from the other end of the hall and realize it's Ryan. He's talking to someone inside a guest room, his back to the hallway.

"Hey!" I say, coming up behind him.

Ryan jumps and slams the door closed. "What the fuck, Beth? Are you trying to give me a heart attack?" His face is red and angry.

"No, my gosh, sorry! I heard you talking to someone and thought I'd come say hi," I say.

"There's no one staying in this room, Beth," he says, twisting the doorknob and pushing the door open. "See? I think you're imagining things. Did you have too many cocktails?"

I look into the room, a room very similar to the one I'm staying in down the hall. He's right; it seems like no one is there.

"No, I'm fine. You're right; nobody is in here," I say, backing out of the room. "Sorry for scaring you. I'll go on down and join the others."

"Good idea," he says. He seems to have calmed down. "I'll be there in a minute."

Downstairs, I locate the spacious dining room. The room

has dark wood beams spanning the ceiling, a large sparkling chandelier, a glowing fireplace, and, of course, all my sorority sisters, who turn and look my way as if they're startled to see me. The space is anchored by an oversized, dark mahogany table, evoking the elegance of the Roaring Twenties. High-backed, carved wooden dining chairs surround it. A large, ornate mirror with a gilded frame reflects the room's ambiance and its sparkling occupants. I'm completely underdressed, of course.

"Mom," Celeste says, appearing by my side, "you look beautiful."

"Don't be silly," I say, feeling my cheeks blush. "But you, my darling, look exquisite."

"Oh, stop it," Celeste says, spinning around. "You like it? Zach picked it out and bought it for me. I feel like a princess." The silver gown is simple, hugging her perfect figure like a glove. A diamond solitaire sparkles at her neck.

"Love it," I say. I want to say please don't become spoiled, please remember who you are, where you came from, which will be hard in the midst of all of this. Celeste wants to be an attorney. I certainly hope she doesn't give up that dream. She can have both, although I wonder if Roxy would be OK with Celeste as a working woman, not just a socialite housewife.

Celeste squeezes my hand and pulls me into the room. The long table is set with place mats and china; arrangements of white roses and greens spill out of crystal vases lining the center of the table. All of this for Zach and Celeste's engagement party. Night one. A restored fireplace with decorative tile adds a cozy, warm touch to the room. I take a deep breath and try to appreciate the surroundings, if not the company. When Ryan enters the room, Roxy comes to life.

"Now that everyone is here," Roxy says, clinking a champagne flute with her fork, "let's please take our seats. You'll find your name card easily." I roll my eyes. Only Roxy would insist on name cards and assigned seats for a party of this size.

Roxy has changed into a vibrant blue full-length dress whose color, I notice, matches the silk place mats. It's like she designed the table around herself, which I'm sure she did. Unfortunately, I must admit the effect is stunning.

"Beth, dear, you're over here by me," Amelia says, waving from the other side of the table. I'm used to being the odd man out, so to speak. For a moment in time, Celeste was my partner in crime. But now, she's found her love and I'm back to just me. I'd better get used to it again.

11

BETH

I make my way around the huge dining room table.

"Be right there," I say, although I don't relish the notion of sitting next to Amelia. Sure, she's a grieving widow, I suppose, and a newly single mom, which should leave us with plenty to talk about for a change, but I still don't have anything to say to her. Celeste is taking her seat at the head of the table, farthest from where I am seated. I want my daughter back.

"Hey, Ms. Harris," Zach says, pulling out my chair for me. "You look lovely tonight."

"Thanks, Zach," I say. Remember, he's a great boy. Don't judge a kid by his mother; that's the golden rule. "It's Beth, please. Call me Beth. Oh, good. You're sitting next to me."

"I am." Zach takes his seat at the head of the table.

"So, dear Beth," Amelia says, slurring her words and stumbling around a bit because I know she wanted to insert the word "poor" before my name. I guess Roxy hadn't been exaggerating in her sly references to Amelia always having a drink in her hand. "How are you anyway? You work for some nonprofit or something? Sounds…interesting."

I take a deep breath. "It is, actually. Our organization builds low-income housing for families. We're about to break ground on a huge development, and I am so excited. We are taking donations, of course. As a mom, I'm sure you understand the need," I say. A server brings around a tray of what appear to be martinis, and I wave her over. Somehow, I've already finished my glass of champagne. This is going to be a long night.

"Right, I am sadly a single mom now, again. I'm sure you all remember that I married my second husband, the wealthy one, Senator Dell, after I had my first kid with the horrible husband," Amelia says.

I vaguely remember she had a short, fiery marriage after college. "Luckily, I met Dick, and the rest, as they say, is a beautiful dream," Amelia says. "Until he died, rest his soul." She puts her hands together in a prayer gesture before putting a finger to her lips, red fingernail shiny and sharp, before letting out a cackle.. "Who am I kidding? I'm so damn lucky. Dick left me rich."

"Well good for you," Brett says, leaning onto Amelia's shoulder. "And gorgeous too."

"Why, thank you, you charmer," Amelia says, kissing Brett on the cheek.

"And Beth, you look lovely, and Jamie, well, all of you ladies. How lucky am I to be here?" Brett says.

This will be the longest dinner ever. I look around the table and spot Jamie rolling her eyes at Amelia's flirtation. A kindred soul, of sorts, I suppose. She always worked hard at classes during college; she was driven to become a doctor, and she did it. I'm a little surprised Jamie was invited here this weekend, actually. She was a year behind us in school and always seemed too nice to belong to the Roxy-Amelia crew, even though she was Roxy's sorority little sister. I sense someone watching me and look up to find Ryan giving me a sheepish smile. He clinks his fork against his still full champagne glass. Maybe he's planning to apologize for overreacting upstairs?

"I'd like to propose a toast to get this little weekend started. First, to Celeste and Zach, may the love you have now grow stronger every moment. To Roxy, for bringing us all together here. And to Beth, welcome to the family. It's almost like fate wanted us all to be together again, and here we are," he says. "Cheers."

I raise my martini glass, embarrassed I've finished my champagne, and clink Ryan's glass before we cheer all around. And with that, the salad course is served. At least everyone will have something to focus on other than each other. Zach, who is seated next to his mother, is in deep conversation with Roxy. To my left, Amelia and Brett are giggling like schoolchildren. Across the table, Ryan eats his salad. I want to ask him why he bought this place, this old mansion that looks so much like the Desert Sunrise. Why would he want a vacation home that constantly reminds him of—.

"Ryan, Zach has a good thought about the rehearsal dinner location," Roxy says, as if sensing I was about to ask Ryan a question myself. Although rehearsal dinners are traditionally the purview of the groom's family, and weddings are the bride's family, Roxy already commandeered the wedding. She can't have everything, can she? Roxy smiles at me.

Maybe it's just as well she changed the subject to all these wedding plans. There are some subjects too painful to revisit. And what happened in the desert all those years ago is one of them.

"I'd like to host the rehearsal dinner," I say. "It will be simple, but it's the least I can do since your family is generously handling the wedding."

Zach and Roxy both look like I've suddenly ripped all my clothes off in front of them. What's the word? *Aghast.*

"That's really sweet, Ms. Harris," Zach says, despite the fact I've asked him to call me Beth. "But Mom and I agree that having it at the yacht club would be perfect."

And I'm not a member, of course.

"Celeste," I say, looking down the huge table at my daughter, "is that what you want? The yacht club for rehearsal dinner?" I watch as my daughter locks eyes with her fiancé, who smiles at her like they have many secrets between them already.

"Mom, it's a great space," my daughter says. The future Mrs. Gentry wants her rehearsal dinner at the yacht club. I'm out of my league.

I wish I hadn't finished my champagne.

"Well, good," Roxy says. "That's settled. Of course, we'll give you a tour of the space before the big night, so you'll feel comfortable, Beth."

I ignore Roxy and instead stare off into the corner of the room, admiring the built-in bar, its ornate glassware and decanters reflecting the flickering light from the fireplace. I'll never be comfortable with this situation, none of it.

12

AMELIA

Brett is doing his best to help me remember why I don't like men. I take a sip of what must be my fourth or fifth glass of pinot grigio, a fine vintage, I suppose, but I can barely taste it anymore. Roxy does have exquisite taste and an unlimited budget, so I never complain about her choice in wine.

I turn to my so-called date and flash what my recently deceased husband calls my killer smile. He did not mean that in a good way. He meant, if looks could kill, he'd be dead. Oh, and now I guess that is true. Rest in peace, Senator. We were, truth be told, about to announce our divorce when he died. I know he planned to murder me slowly by stretching out our separation and divorce proceedings, trying to keep every last dime from me that he could. Meanwhile, I was doing my best to turn all four kids against him. But then he died, and our marriage, seemingly intact, can live on in infamy as a model for all times. Ironic, really, the timing of everything. And now I get to spend all his old money. Perfect.

I stare at Brett, who for some reason is complimenting Beth's hair. He'll be sorry he's acting this way. In New England, we raise men to be attentive to their dates and no one else. I take a deep breath, rub my pearls between my fingertips.

"Brett, could you pour me another glass of wine?" I say through gritted teeth. I've had about enough of him spending all his time charming Beth, who is irritatingly pretty, although she doesn't seem to know it, and always single. Fortunately, Beth doesn't seem interested in my date, nor does Jamie, sitting across the table. Every time Brett compliments her or starts a dinner-party friendly conversation and asks her opinion, Jamie grabs her husband's arm like she's about to be attacked. The poor girl is as shy as she's always been. And try as he may, Brett also has failed to win Roxy over; that much is clear.

"Here you go! You've finished the bottle," Brett says to me after he's poured my glass. "Impressive tolerance."

"Oh, I'm not that tolerant," I say. I grab my steak knife and slice a bite of beef tenderloin and pop it into my mouth. Very tender, melts in your mouth. Why does Roxy always have the best of everything? It's not fair.

"Attention, you all," Roxy says, clinking her glass with a shiny silver spoon.

Oh God, another toast. Is it going to be like this all weekend? Perhaps they'll all run out of things to say? Not likely.

"I want to tell you all how much it means to me that we could

all be together again in such a joyous celebration of young love,"
Roxy says. "While I could have simply invited you all to one of
the many future parties I've planned to celebrate this couple, it
seemed important to have an intimate time with just us sorority
sisters. I mean, once Zach and Celeste found each other, it was
fate—like their job was to bring us back together again. I'm so
happy to be the one to facilitate this weekend. And I did pick
this place on purpose. To give us a chance to be together for a
whole weekend, under one roof. Our Newport Beach house isn't
this intimate. And even though I'd never been to this home, I
knew Ryan had created something special here."

She nods toward Ryan as she holds her glass up high. I think
she is going to finally have us toast, but instead she smiles and
keeps talking. Darn it. "It seems like only yesterday we were
all so young ourselves, with so much potential and life in front
of us. And what an overdue reunion, y'all. We haven't stayed
together under one roof since college. We were so close back
then—sisters, truly, through and through. I love each and every
one of you, and I'm pinching myself that we get to be together
this weekend."

I like her dress, and her diamonds are sparkling like crazy.
I'll up my game tomorrow night, I think, noticing this black silk
dress looks a lot like the navy linen dress I had on today. Oh,
darn it. I drifted off, and now I'm back and she's still talking.

"And I know we'll make new memories to carry us through
to the next reunion. Oh, and that next reunion will likely be
soon at some of the other events I'm planning for Celeste and

Zach, if you all haven't had enough celebrating. Can we ever have too much of Theta Gamma Mu sisters? Of course not."

I look across the table and notice Ryan is trying to get Roxy's attention. But she's rambling about each of the upcoming wedding events like she's in some kind of event planner daze. This must be the highlight of her life, and we're all props in her wedding show.

"So, let's raise a glass to Theta Gamma Mu, the sorority that brought us all together and made us sisters," Roxy says. "Cheers!"

As Roxy sits, Ryan excuses himself, holding his phone in the air. "I'll be right back."

I watch Roxy's expression tumble into a frown, but when she catches me watching her, she plasters a big, white-toothed grin on her face.

I smile. I love seeing masks slip. And isn't that really what sorority life was all about? Keeping the mask on, tight. At least that's what my momma always said.

"You know what was the best part of sorority life? When Jamie became my little sister. Jamie, you and I seemed like opposites, but in fact we grew close. I have such fond memories of our time in the sorority together," Roxy says, ignoring me as well as her husband's abrupt departure.

I half-expect Jamie to refute the question—the expression on her face since she got here has hardly been that of someone who's reliving happy memories. "It is pretty remarkable that we all came from different parts of the country, with totally different pasts, and suddenly, we're all thrown together and told we are sisters," Jamie says. "I'm surprised it works, but it has for all these generations of Theta Gamma Mus."

"That's because we rush well. We know the type we're looking for," Roxy says, slipping into her former role as sorority president like a well-worn leather glove. "We almost always picked right, and when we didn't, remember, there were ways of getting the misfits to deactivate."

I rather enjoyed it when the gals all turned on someone. Great theater, I must say.

"The misfits hid so well sometimes that you didn't really see them until you'd already let them in," I say.

"Yes, you're right, Amelia," Jamie says, pushing a strand of hair behind her ear. "But that didn't happen often. Do you remember that song, our chapter's song? We should sing it now."

Roxy says, "What was that phrase in the old Theta Gamma song we used to sing? 'The unbreakable bond is there yesterday, today, and tomorrow.'"

"Yes, that's it," Jamie says. "'Sisters, sisters, yesterday, today, and tomorrow.' I loved that song. I loved all of you too. I really did."

13

JAMIE

"This is what I needed," I say as everyone around the table watches me. "Sisters. I never had any of my own, and well, you all filled that hole in my life."

Greer leans over and kisses my cheek. He's so sweet. I wonder if he's picking up on the Amelia versus Roxy show. Maybe he's enjoying this fabulous meal, dining in this amazing room. Roxy and Ryan are so lucky.

Really, we're all so lucky. I look around the table and watch as Celeste and Zach lean together and share a secret. Likely making fun of all the old sorority memories. When Celeste sits back up, I'm struck again by her similarity to Sunny. It's uncanny.

My phone buzzes in my pocket. It's my duty nurse. I need to take this call.

"Excuse me for a moment. I have a patient who is in the

ICU. They have a question about meds," I say and hurry out of the dining room, finding a quiet spot in the hallway.

I call Sandra and she fills me in on the patient's vitals. I advise her on the best treatment options and tell her to call me if anything changes.

I decide to head back to our room for a moment, grab something, before returning to dinner. With the Roxy and Amelia show on full display, I likely won't be missed.

14

AMELIA

Jamie has returned and leans against Greer, a smile on her face for the first time since she got here. She seems so full of love for her sisters at the moment. It's all enough to make me want to vomit.

It's such a lie. What is wrong with these people? I wonder, looking around the dining room table. It's all a bunch of baloney.

"Those sisterly bonds weren't so unbreakable for Sunny, were they?" I ask.

I know I'm drunk, and I may be slurring my words, but they all heard me. Someone had to mention the elephant in the room. I mean, it's ridiculous. I'm fed up with people tiptoeing around the subject of Sunny while being all rah-rah sorority reunion-ish. I mean, this house looks like the Desert Sunrise, so of course Sunny's on all our minds. How could she not be? It's almost as if she's here with us in this room.

I take a moment to look each of them in the eye, those who will meet mine, that is. This room sparkles with opulence and is an overwhelming display of privilege. Sure, yes, I can appreciate such things since I grew up having the finest of everything and expect it still today. But what I don't understand is this veil of denial we've all chosen to wear. It's as if the bad thing happened but we refuse to acknowledge its ripple effect. Well, I don't. I know what Sunny's death meant for me. I don't think any of these people think about that, though.

"You do all realize that all our lives changed when she died," I say. "That is the truth of it."

The atmosphere in the room shifts again as the lively chatter they were resuming has been interrupted by my pronouncement. Yes, they're all watching me now, a mixture of fear and anger visible on their faces. Beth's face is frozen in an open-mouthed gasp. There is an air of tension now lingering over all of us like an unspoken question.

Of course, Roxy, the hostess with the mostest, will try to shift the conversation, likely to herself, if I had to guess. I've disrupted the carefully orchestrated ambiance of the dinner.

"Amelia, there's no need to bring those bad memories up, not here, not this weekend," Roxy says. "Not in front of the kids."

Everyone wants me to drop the subject. The room hangs in a delicate balance, awaiting the next ripple of the drama to unfold. And I'm gladly the one to do it.

"Well, Roxy," I say, "this involves *the kids,* as you call them, directly. If Sunny hadn't died at a resort in the desert, Beth wouldn't have married the first loser who came along." I pause and flash my signature smile. It's my sorority smile turned mom smile turned congressional spouse power look. A lips-pursed smile. I clutch my pearls.

"Amelia!" Beth says. She stares at me as if she wants to punch me. She wouldn't; she couldn't no matter what I say or do. She's a tiny mouse, the poor mouse, always has been. I feel her daughter's stare too. Now, that Celeste, I can tell she's stronger than her mom, and she's marrying into some big money, so she'll be set for life. But I don't care. I'm right about this.

"You know it's true, Beth. And you should know that, too, Celeste. Sunny was your mom's best friend. She totally would have talked your mom out of marrying that guy, your loser dad. And once she had talked some sense into you, Beth, well, Celeste, you wouldn't be here," I say.

Beth's face is red with a mixture of embarrassment and anger, but she knows I'm telling the truth, so she doesn't say anything. Celeste looks both surprised and confused. Beth never told her that her best friend, Sunny, died at a desert resort. Strange.

"And you know what else? If Sunny hadn't died, Zachary wouldn't be here either. Isn't that interesting?" I say.

"Amelia, that's enough," Roxy says, eyes narrowing, trying to threaten me with her Roxy powers.

But I'm not finished. "And if Sunny had lived, we wouldn't all be here celebrating their engagement. It's funny how good things arise from tragedy, isn't it?" I look around at their stunned faces. They are acting like I'm speaking in tongues when, really, I'm telling the truth.

I hold up my glass of wine, woefully almost empty. "I'd like to make a toast. To Sunny. Your death brought Roxy and me closer together. I cannot even begin to imagine how different my life might be without her friendship and support all these years. To Sunny, and to Roxy. Cheers!"

The others finally raise their glasses after an awkward pause. They're such cowards, so easily silenced and scared. As we clink our glasses together, I'm pleased to see that Roxy's mask has fallen completely now, and her benevolent smile doesn't quite hide the distress in her eyes.

15

BETH

That was the world's longest dinner, I think as I make my way down the hallway to my room. I'm glad my room is at the end of the hall, as far away as possible from Roxy, who has a huge suite of rooms at the other end of the hall that she has dubbed "The G Suite." Amelia and Brett are in the pool house, apart from the rest of us. Obviously, that was a good call. How awkward to end the evening on her distasteful toast to Sunny. All those things Amelia said still weigh heavily on my heart, and I've been on edge ever since. I open the door to the room and step inside.

"Mom," Celeste says, and I jump like I saw a ghost.

"Oh my gosh, I didn't hear you behind me," I say, my hand covering my rapidly beating heart. I find the light switch and turn on the chandelier over the bed, an elegant illumination to the entire room.

"Obviously," she says. "Sorry I scared you. Can I come in?"

"Of course, honey," I say and hurry to close the door behind her. I have the creeps, and her unexpected appearance doesn't help. But I am glad to see her—of course I am. I need to calm down. "Shouldn't you be heading to bed? You have another big day tomorrow."

"Unfortunately," she says. "Mom, I'm so sorry."

"For what?" I ask. "You haven't done anything wrong, my perfect girl." Except the whole getting engaged too soon and the yacht club thing, but really, she's young and a yacht club sounds, well, Gentry-like. "Don't look so sad. I'll get over the yacht club decision. I need to get used to the new reality."

"No, it's not that. We haven't decided anything about the rehearsal dinner. And I want you involved, so ignore Mrs. Gentry when she says things like that."

"Mrs. Gentry? Aren't you supposed to call her Mom?" I say.

"Please, there's only one woman in my life who has earned the Mom title, and that's you, period," she says. "So, you ignore her too. OK?"

"Ignore Roxy? Gladly," I say with a smile. "So, what is it, darling? What could you possibly have to be sorry for?"

"I'm sorry I didn't know that this desert house was so like the hotel where your best friend died. That's why everyone's been acting so weird today, right? I really had no idea, Mom," she says and sits on the bed.

I walk to the fireplace and flip the switch, welcoming the warmth and the cozy light.

"I know, I understand, I really do. You've never been here

before and even if you had been, you never saw the Desert Sunrise. I'm sure Roxy talked you into having your engagement weekend here, with Zach's help," I say. I join her on the bed. I can't help but wonder if Roxy has some ulterior motive for gathering us all in this place that's so reminiscent of the hotel where tragedy struck all those years ago. Maybe it's one of Roxy's mind games, making us uneasy to make herself feel like she's in control.

Celeste has clasped her hands together in her lap, a frown marring her beautiful face. She takes my hand in hers and says, "Yes, I didn't have a say in the matter. Zach and his mom picked this place to hold the weekend. I don't even think Mr. Gentry wanted it here."

"He does seem off, and he disappears a lot," I say. "Like he doesn't want us here, but then he sort of does. It's all strange. We need to get through tomorrow, and then we'll get out of here."

Celeste smiles and then takes a deep breath. "Look, Mom, I know you don't like to talk about Sunny. All you've ever told me is that your best friend died during your senior year of college. I never knew anything about a desert hotel. But if you'd like to talk about it, about her, I'm here to listen."

I wrap my arms around my daughter and pull her close to me. Her hair is the same length as Sunny's was, but Celeste's is a mixture of yellows, some bright, some dark, depending on how much sunshine she is exposed to. Sunny was a white blond, with gorgeous emerald-green eyes. Sunny was known for wearing green dresses and shirts in all shades of the color to make her eyes pop even more. I remember the last dinner, the last night of spring break. I was dressed in borrowed going-out clothes, borrowed from Sunny, of course, and I felt I looked about as sexy as I ever would in a tight white T-shirt and short red skirt. I expected Sunny to appear at any moment wearing a signature green dress and a big smile. I shake my head to push away the memory, but I cannot stop the images from flooding in.

I spotted our group already seated at the Desert Sunrise's outdoor restaurant, off the lobby of the hotel. Ryan saw me first and waved. I joined him and Jamie at the table.

"You're looking really good tonight, Beth," Ryan said, his smile looking whiter than usual with his tanned face.

"Thank you," I said, feeling my face flush. I pulled out a chair next to Jamie, who already was halfway finished with her Sunrise Margarita, the specialty drink of the hotel.

"You better hurry and catch up," she said, winking as she took another big sip. "I'm going to miss doing this every day and night."

"Probably better for our livers that the vacation is almost over," Ryan said, waving the waiter over. "Two more of those, please."

"Oh, I think I'll have beer tonight," I said.

"Aw, come on, Beth. This is our last night," Ryan said. "Bring her a Sunrise Margarita, double tequila."

I laughed and shrugged my shoulders. It was our last night. The entire week of spring break had been like this—warm weather, friendly conversations over too many drinks, and memories to last a lifetime. Our margaritas arrived at the same time as Roxy and

Amelia, both wearing fitted short dresses, Roxy's with gold sequins and Amelia's all white and almost transparent.

"Wowza, ladies," Ryan said. "You both clean up nice."

"You don't look too terrible yourself, Ryan," Roxy said. She kissed him on the cheek, leaning over to exhibit her ample cleavage, before sliding into the seat next to him. I always did find it obnoxious how much Roxy flirted with Sunny's longtime boyfriend. Sunny always laughed it off, saying that's how Roxy was, but it would drive me crazy. Not Sunny, though. Sunny had all the confidence in the world.

"Hey, where's Sunny?" Ryan asked.

I had been wondering the same thing, expecting her to appear at our table at any moment.

"Oh, she's going to go to sleep early tonight. All that day drinking, I suppose. Check your texts she said she'd tell you her plans," Roxy said with a grin. "Oh, waiter, we'll have two more of those, and some chips and salsa. It's our last night so we should make it a night to remember."

I look at the fireplace flickering in the corner of the bedroom, and I'm back in the present, sitting beside my daughter, talking about my best friend, but I can't help being lost in the memory of that night, still torn apart by the choices I made, the things I did and didn't do.

"Mom? Are you OK?" Celeste says.

"I'm fine," I say. But I'm not.

16

BETH

"Mom?" Celeste says and squeezes my hand. "Tell me what happened to Sunny."

"Most of the people who were there that spring break are here, at Gentry House, except for Greer and Brett," I say. I sweep my hand. "This room isn't like our hotel rooms back then, of course. It's much nicer, but it feels similar to the Desert Sunrise, where we stayed. The art deco lines coupled with the Spanish textures, it's an overwhelming feeling with every step on the Spanish tile floor."

"I'm sorry, Mom," she says.

Should I tell her the air seems charged with unspoken tension? It has since I arrived. I don't want to upset her further. Besides, Celeste's attempt to help me through it is making it worse. And despite Ryan's pricy renovation of this place, I can't shake the ghostly connection to the past. I feel trapped in a complex intersection of conflicting emotions—a place that is both familiar and foreign, comforting and distressing.

I look into Celeste's kind blue eyes and take a deep breath. "Nobody saw Sunny at all the last night of spring break," I say. "She'd told Roxy and Amelia before dinner that she was too tired to party that night and that she was going to go to sleep early."

"OK," Celeste says. "Was Sunny like that, responsible? I mean, most college seniors keep partying no matter how tired they are, and it was the last night of your trip."

"I know, but she made that choice. Very responsible. She knew how to have fun, too, but she was, yes, responsible. She wouldn't want any of us to take care of her or change her plans; she'd want us to enjoy our last night," I say. "So we all thought she was asleep. But at some point in the middle of the night, she must have left her hotel room and gone outside. Maybe she was hungry or thirsty; we don't know."

I sigh and take a deep breath.

"It's OK, Mom, if you don't want to tell me anything more tonight," Celeste says, wrapping her arm around me.

But now that I've started, it's like I can't stop. "Somehow, Sunny ended up walking out near the pool. All our rooms opened out onto it, like here," I say. "Except here, the bedrooms are on the second floor; at least mine is. But at the Desert Sunrise, we were all on the first floor with easy pool access. She must have slipped and fallen in."

"Oh my gosh," Celeste says. "No wonder you're so tense and anxious today. This place must be so triggering."

All I can do is nod. "The hotel staff found her face down in the pool the next morning, with a big gash on the side of her head." I take a deep, ragged breath. "The coroner told us she must have hit her head when she slipped and knocked herself unconscious. They think she drowned without ever waking up."

"Poor Sunny. That is so horrible," Celeste says. "I'm so sorry, Mom."

"I'm the sorry one. I've always blamed myself for not checking on Sunny after dinner that night. It would have been easy for me to go check on her, bring her dinner so she would have something to eat before we all went out for the night. Maybe she was hungry, looking for food when she fell," I say. I know the guilt will never end.

"Mom, that's not your fault. You were having fun; you all were," Celeste says. "No one could have known this accident would happen."

"I don't know if fun is even the word for it. After dinner, Amelia insisted on dragging Jamie and me to the casino nearby to hang out with some cute guys she'd met earlier that day. Amelia was the consummate flirt. She and Roxy had a competition of sorts back in the day," I say. "And of course, as soon as we got there, she ditched us, snuck off with one of the guys while the others were buying us drinks. She's a piece of work, that one. Always has been."

"I can tell," Celeste says, clearly unimpressed with Amelia after her little toast at dinner.

"You have to take everything she says with a grain of salt, or ignore it, please. As they say, you never can trust a politician. I think it must apply to the spouses too. She must be a natural in DC," I say. "But that night, I agreed to go along with her plan. I'll always wonder what would have happened if I hadn't."

"It's not your fault, Mom, what happened to Sunny. You were young, it was spring break, you're supposed to be out, flirting with guys," Celeste says. "You were doing what everybody does on spring break senior year in college. Nothing is your fault."

I look at my beautiful daughter and manage a smile.

"Thank you for saying that, honey," I say.

"Thank you for telling me everything finally," Celeste says. She stands and stretches. "I do think it's past my bedtime. Are you going to be all right?"

"Yes, sure, and it is late. You need your beauty sleep," I say. I want to ask her how she and Zach are doing but decide to wait until tomorrow. I'll be watching them in action.

"Unless you want to tell me anything else. You know I'm always here for you," she says.

"Likewise, for you," I say and stand to give her a hug. "You know everything now. I love you."

She nods and walks toward the door. "Good night, Mom. See you in the morning."

I take a deep breath and close and lock the door behind her, dropping my head. The fact is I lied to my daughter. She doesn't need to know about the one-night stand that followed the evening at the casino, that last night of spring break. There are some things a daughter doesn't need to know about her mother.

I walk into the bathroom and stare at my reflection in the mirror. I cannot escape myself, or the guilt from that night. Because while I was enjoying a spring break hookup, my best friend was drowning, all alone.

17

AMELIA

The air is hot and tropical already this morning as Brett and I walk hand in hand through the landscaped grounds and past the pool to the main house, where everyone else is staying. We're the outcasts, and I like it that way.

Of course, a wave of déjà vu washes over me seeing the pool, with the same type of mosaic tile as the pool where Sunny died. But that's fine, I can handle it. It's not the same pool, and I'm glad Roxy shoved Brett and me out here in the doghouse. It's for the best, of course; our wild lovemaking would have disturbed these vanilla types.

"Fun time last night," I say as we step inside the main house. I must admit I did appreciate his physical agility last night. By the end, my husband had let himself go. Likely what did him in.

"Oh yeah, it was," Brett says with a big grin on his face. "More fun tonight?"

"Count on it," I say.

We walk into the kitchen to find a buffet set up on the island, reminiscent of what you'd find in a fine hotel: scrambled eggs, bacon, sausage, bagels, cream cheese, smoked salmon, capers, avocado toast, and a green salad. A feast.

Jamie and Greer are seated at the kitchen table, already enjoying it.

"Morning, you two," I say as Brett and I grab plates.

"Good morning," Greer says.

I notice Jamie isn't smiling and seems enraptured by building her bagel and cream cheese. I guess she's mad at me too. Whatever. It's been a minute since Jamie and I have caught up, and we certainly drifted apart after college. I've watched her, though, through social media and her annual Christmas cards. She's always been so busy with her perfect family, her career as a cardiologist, and the countless charity boards she sits on. Besides, it's not like we were ever all that close. She was a whole year younger than all of us, and mostly we tolerated her in our inner circle because Roxy had chosen her as her little sister.

I'm still not sure why. There were certainly better choices, more connected and wealthy choices, for sure. Jamie was always so uptight; even during rush you could see it. The notion of party-girl Roxy mentoring and taking under her wing the no-fun Jamie, well, I'd tried to talk her out of it. But when Roxy makes her mind up, you can't ever change it.

"Stop trying to change my mind," Roxy had said when I'd suggested other alternatives. "I'm what Jamie needs. She needs to lighten up. Have some fun, and who better to teach her than yours truly. Am I right? Besides, I don't want any competition from my little sis. And she's, well, wholesome enough to not steal my thunder, if you know what I mean. These young girls are a threat." She tossed her blond hair over her shoulder.

"No, they are not, not for you. You're untouchable. And you should pick someone else," I'd said. But it turns out, they did have a solid bond. I wouldn't say Roxy made Jamie into a party girl, she was much too busy studying for that, but the two of them have stayed friendly over the years, and that's more than I can say about my little sister. I don't even remember her name now. Ha.

Beside me, Brett says, "They even made fresh-squeezed orange juice. I feel like I'm at a five-star resort."

I smile. I wouldn't expect anything less from Roxy. "You are. Hotel Roxy."

We carry our plates over to the table and join Jamie and Greer.

"So, Jamie—is it OK if I call you Jamie, or would you prefer Dr. Vale? I hear you're the top cardiologist in Orange County," Brett says, taking a big bite of eggs.

Greer looks up and tilts his head. The wrinkles next to his eyes make him look his age, unlike the rest of us who get rid of those the minute they appear, including Brett. "How did you know Jamie is a cardiologist?"

"Oh, I'm a pharmacist," Brett says. "In my job you get to know a lot of doctors' names, since you're filling prescriptions for their patients. But it's always nice to put a face to the name."

"Makes sense," Greer says. "My wife is a star, that's for sure. Her practice is full; she's even thinking about going concierge. People will pay thousands of dollars to be one of her patients."

Jamie smiles without looking up, continuing to be very busy with her bagel. It's almost like she isn't here at the table with us. She's acting so shy and modest after her husband's bragging about how kick-ass she is. If anybody ever bragged about me that way, I'd be jumping for joy.

Brett says, "You know, Jamie, after breakfast, I'd love to pick your brain if you have a minute. I need to figure out this drug interaction one of my customers keeps having. It could be deadly, and I didn't spot it."

"Now, now. I didn't bring you here to talk about drug interactions; I brought you here for fun," I say. I am sick of him paying attention to Jamie. "You should focus on making your date happy."

"Oh, I did that last night, remember?" he says.

Don't flatter yourself, I want to say, but I'm distracted. These eggs are melting in my mouth—how did they make them so perfect?—and the avocado toast is the best I've ever had. Roxy must have had a team in the kitchen putting all this together.

"You know, come to think of it, I remember you from chemistry class, Jamie," Brett says.

"Wow, that was a long time ago," I say. "I thought you only remembered me."

"Mostly you, Amelia, of course," he says. "But, Jamie, I think I was your TA one semester. Organic Chemistry? You probably would've been a junior. I think that's when most students took that class."

Jamie shakes her head. "I'm afraid I don't remember that class at all. That whole year was a blur, actually." I watch as she pushes her plate away, clearly uncomfortable with the topic.

I wonder why?

18

AMELIA

Greer puts his arm around his wife. "Jamie's whole life had led to being president of Theta Gamma Mu," he explains to the room. "She worked hard to make sure she could step into her mother's legacy as chapter president. She earned straight A's in pre-med and did the whole sorority thing with you guys. That's a lot for anyone. A ton of pressure, but of course, she came through. She's something else, this wife of mine, but you all already know that. You're her sisters."

I smile my tight-lipped power smile and watch their interaction. Interesting. "I'd forgotten you were the next chapter president, after Roxy, who was ours. I can only imagine what a tight ship you ran," I say. I mean, Jamie barely even went to any of our chapter functions. Roxy had to beg her to come to spring break with us, not that the rest of us really wanted her there. I guess she wanted to be sure she always had a loyal acolyte around her, even on spring break. And Jamie certainly was one. "Hopefully you let the girls have some fun, now and then too."

And now I remember why Roxy insisted on being her big sister: Jamie was a huge legacy, and that's why she got the bid to join Theta Gamma Mu, despite the lack of what we used to call "sparkle and shine." Jamie had neither. When I think back on that first recruitment I'd been part of as an active, I still remember all those smiling, nervous faces. So many girls, many with the sparkle that we said we looked for and did. But we also looked for something else. The chapter meetings always included profiles of the top rushees, and Jamie was at the top of our pile.

Which didn't make any sense to me. I had a number of quality picks who would add more life, more class, and more clout to Theta Gamma Mu. Jamie was shy, bookish, and didn't seem all that interested in being in the sorority.

"Look at this résumé," the chapter president at the time had said during a rush meeting. "This one, Jamie Vale, is a double legacy. But not only that, her mother was chapter president of this very chapter, and so was her grandmother. I've never even heard of it."

I'd raised my hand. I was only a sophomore, and I knew I didn't have any power, but I had principles.

"Yes, Amelia?" the president said.

"I'm wondering why legacy matters more than personality or, say, money," I asked. "The chapter is always raising money. I'd recruit with that in mind first."

"That is one of many considerations we look for, of course,

but we don't discriminate based on a recruit's parents' ability to give a big endowment," she said to me as a murmur washed through the room.

I knew what my sisters were whispering. I got a bid to Theta Gamma Mu for that very reason, guaranteed. I smiled.

"Well, personality should count. Jamie Vale isn't memorable. She seems better suited to Alpha Beta Boring," I said. "But you are sold on her?"

"We are. Now, let's go over our next top recruit," the president said, pulling out another resume. And just like that, I knew we'd welcome Jamie Vale into Theta Gamma Mu, despite the fact she didn't belong.

But that didn't matter. She had quite a family legacy. Quite the expectations from them, too, I imagine.

I'm glad I'd graduated and had not had to deal with President Jamie. Roxy had been enough. More than enough.

"It was a big job, and an honor, of course," Jamie agrees, twisting some strands of her blond hair around a finger, before tucking it behind her ear. "Roxy was a great mentor."

"I'm sure you did a great job," Brett says, smiling at her like she's the queen bee.

She's not. What does he know about anything? He wasn't there, wasn't in our sorority, didn't even know Jamie. He's doing that annoying flirting thing again. I sneer at him, willing him to shut up. He glances at me and seems to get the memo.

"I'm sure you were a great sorority girl, too, Amelia," he says. "Those cute red-haired pigtails you wore. Adorable."

I roll my eyes, but I enjoy his attention on me. "Yes, I went through a phase, unfortunately," I say. "But sure, I was a fantastic member of Theta Gamma Mu. Everyone knows that."

That's not especially true, but I was there. I saw it all. I'm a watcher. It's my superpower. And I also like to have fun. When you're going through sorority rush, though, it's all fake. I mean, sure, there are secret rush dates, and you can sort of make a connection, but it's all a performance. There is an endgame, and that is getting in the sorority, whatever it takes. So it changes the meaning of friendship, at least until you're invited in. Friends become sisters, they say. But really, it's desperate strangers become sisters, and then some of us become friends. It's the way it works, always has, always will.

I'm sure Jamie's reign was no fun, and I'm lucky I graduated before she became president. But it's not like Roxy was a stellar president either. I mean, look at what she did to Sunny.

19

ROXY

Ryan walks out of the master bath dressed and ready for the day. It's annoying how much he's avoiding me. I've barely had a chance to wake up.

"See you at breakfast," he says, headed for the door.

"Wait, honey. We've hardly had time to talk since I got here the other day. Stay a minute and catch up with me. Didn't you think last night's dinner was beautiful?" I say, wrapping my robe tighter around my waist.

"Sure, dinner was great," he says.

"Isn't it nice for all of us to be together again?" I ask.

He shakes his head. "I guess."

"I think what you've done architecturally here and what I've done with the accessories and the tablescape really complemented each other. We're the perfect match, as always."

"I'm hungry. I'm going to breakfast," he says.

I walk over and kiss his cheek. He's still as handsome as the day I first laid eyes on him during college.

"So, who looks the best of all the girls?" I ask. "Not Beth, of course; she still looks like, well, Beth. But am I still the prettiest?"

"You know," he says. And then stops.

"What?" I ask. "Did you want to tell me something?"

"No," he says.

"OK, great. Let's enjoy today with our friends, celebrating Zach, in this beautiful architectural treasure you've restored. We're so blessed."

"So blessed," he says. "I'm going to go eat breakfast. I'm assuming you had the staff prepare a feast."

"I did. Can you wait for me? I'll be a minute," I say and hurry into the large changing area and bathroom. It will take me more than a minute to get ready; we both know that.

Ryan peeks his head into my closet. "Look, Roxy, we're over. You know that, right?"

My heart pounds wildly in my chest. This cannot be happening. I can't move my mouth, I can't speak. I drop the silk dress I held in my hand and watch as it slumps onto the floor. My hand shakes.

Ryan says, "I'm only staying through the wedding, for Zach. I'll see you downstairs."

"What?" I stammer, finally finding my voice. This isn't happening. I won't allow it. "No. We're perfect together. I love you. You love me. It's been the two of us since college," I say as panic washes over me. He can't leave me. I can't be alone. I can't be one of those women everyone talks about. *Oh, she's so lonely and over-the-hill, what will she do?* I don't want that pity, those stares. I'll never be in the social pages again. Oh my God. I hurry to Ryan and throw my arms around his neck. I have built my life around this man. What about our dreams, our future? Our past. "We're good together, great even."

Ryan takes my hands and pulls them off his neck like I'm a fly and he's swatting me. "I know what being great with someone feels like. And this, us, this isn't it."

He starts walking to the door again. I will not be treated this way. I mean, look at me. I could have had anyone back then, and I chose him. He won't leave me. I won't allow it.

"Stop right there," I say, my voice calm but dark and filled with rage. "She's always come between us, and she still is. Isn't she? Twenty-five years of marriage, and she still has your loyalty."

Ryan shakes his head, but he doesn't deny it.

"That's right, Ryan. I know why you bought this godforsaken place—the state of ruin it was in when you saw it reminded you of her. You wanted to re-create that place, the Desert Sunrise, so you could be closer to your college sweetheart, the love of your life, right? I mean it's eerie, Ryan, how much this place resembles that old hotel."

"This isn't about Sunny," he says, but I watch his face flush with color. I don't know if it's embarrassment or rage. "This is about us. You never loved me, not like she did. You loved my family's money. You loved what I could provide."

I burst into tears. "That's not true, Ryan. I loved you then, and I love you now. I always have."

Ryan shakes his head.

I'm crying harder now, giving it all I've got. He'll change his mind, he'll stay, he always does. I let the conversation get out of control this time. I'll do better. I have to do better.

His hand is on the doorknob. I've failed to convince him. He's unmoved.

"Roxy," he says, his voice calm, devoid of emotion.

"What?" I manage, shakily.

"I mean it this time," he says, opening the door. "After the wedding, I'm gone."

20

BETH

We're finishing breakfast when Roxy finally appears, sweeping into the kitchen in a bright yellow, attention-seeking tennis dress. Ryan had eaten already. He wasn't dressed like the sun but instead was rather subdued and quiet when he joined us. I'd had a chance to ask him about the article I found under a stack of magazines on the coffee table in my room, and he seemed as surprised as I was. I'd wanted to ask him about it before Zach and Celeste appeared for breakfast.

"Where did you find it?" he'd asked, turning his attention to me with a frown. He'd been distant and distracted since he came to breakfast.

"Below a stack of magazines on the coffee table in my room. It's an article from that day, in the *Palm Springs Register*. About Sunny's death at the Desert Sunrise. There's a picture of her body, covered in a sheet."

"How horrible," Jamie murmured.

I'd been a wreck since I found it this morning. It brought back that morning so clearly in my mind. Jamie seemed haunted by it too. She looked wide-eyed and stared at Ryan.

"That doesn't make any sense," Ryan said. "Do you have it with you?"

"No, it's back in my room. It's creepy," I said.

"I have no idea how it wound up in your room, but feel free to get rid of it," Ryan said. And then he turned back to his breakfast, end of discussion. I had to wonder if he'd saved it all these years and thought that he likely had. I decided not to push it.

The table had fallen silent by the time Roxy showed up. It was obvious that the two of them are a bit out of sync, but I guess hosting all your long-lost so-called friends for a weekend could be a bit taxing on a relationship. I mean, we're just guests, and spending this much time with each other is already getting on my nerves.

Brett and Amelia have been hanging out in the other part of the kitchen, fortunately. There's something that bothers me about him. It seems Amelia might be getting sick of him too. Her arms are folded across her chest as she speaks to him.

Despite my best efforts to ignore his attention, he keeps flirting with Jamie and me, and it's clearly driving Amelia nuts. As soon as I arrived for breakfast, he turned his attention to me, asking why someone as gorgeous as me was still single and all that sort of stuff. I was about to call him on it when Roxy arrived.

His playboy rapport, sports analogies, and sexual innuendos are ridiculous. And Jamie and, clearly, Amelia agree.

Roxy fills her plate at the buffet with exaggerated glee, plopping a pile of eggs onto her plate enough for two people and piling up a stack of bacon. That's so out of character for her. She barely eats. Maybe she and Ryan had a night of romance? Although, I don't get the same vibe of pulsing desire flowing between Roxy and Ryan, not that I ever really felt that with the two of them. Ryan and Sunny, well, that was a different story.

Roxy notices I'm watching her and flashes a smile. To the room at large she says, "I hope everyone slept well. I know I did. It's the desert air. It's so calming, so relaxing." Roxy is practically dancing as she makes her way over to the table. "It makes me fall in love with this place all over again. The way the sun hits the mountains at the perfect angle. You're all glowing sitting there at the table. Paradise."

Despite her Disney princess appearance and speech about her little slice of paradise, Roxy looks off. Puffy even. Hmm. Interesting. She has yet to take a bite from her mountain of eggs or the stack of bacon.

"What's on the agenda for today, Madam President?" I ask. I watch Ryan carry his plate to the sink without saying another word as Roxy sits down. I stand and clear my plate. I'm only able to sit and eat breakfast for so long, no matter how good it tastes. Sorry, Roxy.

"There are so many choices. You can go on a hike, lounge by

the pool, play pickleball. Ryan designed a tennis court that holds two pickleball courts," Roxy says.

Oh brother. I don't play pickleball, but knowing this is a competitive crowd, I have a feeling they'll force me into it.

Jamie is rinsing the dishes at the sink. She turns off the water and hurries to her husband's side. "That sounds fun. Greer and I are a team. We love to play together. But I'm game for a hike first before it gets too hot out."

From across the kitchen, I watch as Amelia points her finger at Brett and says, "You're mine."

"Whatever you say," Brett says as they rejoin the group. "You know I've taught pickleball for the parks and recreation department. I even host pickleball tournaments. You're lucky to have me."

"You're lucky to have *me*," Amelia says, clearly unimpressed by his pickleball prowess.

I watch Roxy walk toward Ryan, but he's moved away from her and is standing next to me at the sink.

Roxy stops halfway to her destination and turns to face the table, smiling stiffly. "I think we need to inject a little fun into our game. New rule: No one can be with their regular partner," she proclaims.

I roll my eyes. I don't have a regular partner, haven't since forever, and Roxy knows that. Leave it to her to let me know I'm inferior in so many ways, including the fact I'm always single.

"In that case, what do you say, Beth? Want to be my partner?" Ryan says, stepping into the awkwardness. "I can't promise we'll win, but I promise we'll have a good time trying."

I smile, showing my dimple. Ryan to the rescue. Roxy's own smile freezes on her face. Brett turns and says, "Jamie, let's be a team. Unlike Ryan, I *can* promise we'll kick their asses. Let's get playing."

Jamie looks at Greer. He says, "Go on, I'm fine. I don't really feel like playing anyway. I have a stomachache. In fact, if you all will excuse me, I'm going to rummage in your bag for some Pepto-Bismol."

"Of course, sure, feel better," Jamie says.

"Let's go," Brett says, shooing Jamie out the door.

"Come on, Beth. This will be fun. A little competition is good for everyone, sometimes at least," Ryan says, touching my arm.

I look at Roxy, her face flushed in anger. I take a deep breath. "Sure, it's just a game," I say. "Let's go play it. Don't worry, Roxy. Ryan and I will lose, and you can jump right into my spot."

Roxy sits down at the kitchen table, and Amelia joins her. As Ryan and I follow Jamie and Brett out into the warm sunshine, I can feel their eyes on us. They don't like this, any of it. For once, the three of us agree.

21

AMELIA

I stare at the pile of food on Roxy's plate. "Are you going to eat anything?"

"Not hungry," she says, leaning back in her chair. "Lost my appetite suddenly."

"Well, you are dressed to play," I say. "Maybe we should? Or, better yet, we could go on a hike?"

"I'd rather not," she says. "Excuse me."

Whatever. I decide to go out to the pickleball court and watch the match. I walk through the lush, mature gardens. Tall, slender palm trees gracefully sway in the gentle desert breeze, casting dappled shadows across the pathway. Cacti and succulents thrive in sunlit corners, their unique shapes and hues adding a touch of desert authenticity to the scene. I must admit, Ryan turned this place into an awe-inspiring home, inside and out. An array of bougainvillea drapes over trellises, their riotous bursts of magenta, fuchsia, and orange providing a striking contrast against the bright blue sky. The fragrance of citrus blossoms hangs in the air, emanating from neatly arranged lemon and orange trees. As I continue walking down the meandering stone pathway, I spot Greer. He's sitting on a lounge chair outside his room.

"Are you sure you don't want to play pickleball? Be my partner?" I ask, waving to get his attention.

"Sorry, Amelia. I'm afraid I don't feel up to it at the moment. I hope you don't mind, but I ate too much for breakfast," Greer says, crinkly-eyeing me and patting his ample stomach. "Maybe this afternoon, assuming Roxy doesn't have other plans for us."

"Sure," I say and walk away. I guess I don't really need to play pickleball. I've never been a natural athlete, truth be told. The way I was raised, girls did school and cotillion, boys did sports. I suppose it worked for me back then. My own girls play tennis like pros. I made sure of it. You can't be well rounded enough these days. Growing up is a competition all of its own. At least it is in the suburbs.

"Oh, hey, lovebirds," I say as Celeste and Zach appear in front of me on the path. As far as the attractive competition, this couple wins.

"Hey," Celeste says. "Gorgeous out here, isn't it?"

"Yes, these gardens are, well, you can tell they've been here a long time," I say. "Are you two playing pickleball with us? I'm looking for a partner."

"I'd like to play," Celeste says. "I've always wanted to try it."

"We discussed this. We are not playing today. Today's plan is to lie out by the pool, work on our tans," Zach says. "We don't get many days like this in Chicago."

"We can get tan playing pickleball," Celeste says. She has a point.

Zach shakes his head and says, "Come on, Celeste. We made a plan; you promised to sit by the pool with me. You know I hate it when you change things."

Hmm. Rather inflexible young man. I thought he was a momma's boy, but now I see he has a little control issue. Interesting. I feel sorry for Celeste. This should be when he is on his best behavior, the time leading up to the wedding.

"Well, now, I don't suppose you do have days like this in Chicago, to tan or play pickleball," I say as a chill tingles my spine. It's just *a pool*, I remind myself, not *the pool*. "Maybe some pickleball later? Have fun and be careful."

Celeste tilts her head at my warning. I know it sounded odd when it slipped out. As they walk away, I look past them to the pool, sparkling in the distance. And I see her. A woman with long blond hair ducking into the landscape by the pool. Sunny? It can't be. I hurry to the pool; the crystalline water is beckoning me. For a split second the hair on my arms stands on end. I'm sure there's some dark shape floating in the water, in the middle of the pool. Oh my God.

I blink and drop into a chaise lounge, dizzy and disoriented. I search the pool again, but it's gone. It's my imagination playing tricks on me, trying to take me back twenty-five years to that terrible discovery. I remember that morning like it happened yesterday.

Ryan slumped down in a lounge chair by the pool at the Desert Sunrise, hungover and miserable and still wearing last night's clothes. On the other side of the pool, a group of emergency medical personnel were in the process of picking up a stretcher. A stretcher with a sheet draped over the body lying on it. Sunny's body.

I wrap my arms around myself. I glance at the pool. There is nobody there, dead or alive. I decide I need company and head back to the tennis courts. As I arrive, I see Brett high-fiving a reluctant Jamie after what must have been a fierce point. All four of the players look sweaty already, and they haven't been playing that long. I guess it is getting hotter outside. My mind keeps drawing me back to the past, to that awful morning.

Pain explodes on my face, snapping me into the present. My cheek and eye sting as I cover my face with my hands and drop to the court.

"What the heck? I have a gala next week! The president will be there! My face!" I yell, tears streaming from my eyes. I don't really have a gala with the president, but I could. I'm that important.

"Oh crap, Amelia. I'm so sorry," Brett says, rushing over to me. "Let me see. Are you OK?"

Jamie and Beth are both by my side. I don't even know who hit the ball.

"Who hit me?" I ask.

"Um, it was Brett. But right now, Amelia, let Jamie take a look at your face," Ryan says. I reluctantly take my hands away and hope for the best.

Brett slammed a ball into my face? I'm going to kill him.

"I was taking my frustration at losing out on the ball, but I didn't realize I was aiming it at you," Brett says. "Sorry."

"I think you're going to be fine, maybe a bruise," Jamie says. "But I'll go get my medical kit, to be sure. It's a game, Brett, but these balls can be dangerous when hit that way."

Brett's face turns red. "I know. I get carried away sometimes. Sorry, all. Sorry especially to you, Amelia. I smacked that ball with too much rage. Let me make it up to you. I'm going to go get some pain pills for you. One of the many benefits of dating a pharmacist."

"I don't think she needs pharmaceuticals, Brett," Jamie says.

"That's kind of funny, coming from you," Brett says with a grin. At her blank look, he adds, "You know, because you're a doctor. Aren't you people usually the first to send your patients to the pharmacy to find a cure for what ails them? I wouldn't have a job if it weren't for you." Brett gives her a wink that I'm sure he thinks is charming. Then his eyes meet mine. "Give me your hand, Amelia, and I'll help you up."

I don't offer him my hand, instead staying seated on the tennis court. He gets the message and trots away. Jamie frowns as she watches him go. She's clearly fed up with him too.

"Don't worry about Brett, Jamie. He's cocky but he's harmless, unless you're his date and then he uses you as target practice," I say. What a jerk. He's flirting with everyone but his date, and has poor sportsmanship too. Frustrating. At least he lost the pickleball match; that makes me happy.

Jamie shakes her head and backs away. "I'll be right back with my kit."

"Ryan and I will stay here with Amelia," Beth says. Like I'm a baby or something. She's sort of sweaty, and I don't want her to drip on me. I scooch to the side, out of her drip range.

"Thanks, Beth. Whatever would I do without you?" I say. She always was a bleeding heart, I remember. Always quick to lend a hand to a sister who needed support. Ironic, considering Beth herself was needier, financially speaking, than almost anyone else in the sorority. Funny how some things haven't changed since college.

My gaze wanders to Jamie's retreating form, her stride brisk and purposeful as she heads toward the house. Speaking of people who haven't changed much. She might be Dr. Vale these days, but she still has a stick up her ass. At least she had some champagne last night. Back at SCU, she never even drank alcohol at the parties, though I wasn't sure if that was because she was a scrupulous rule follower or because she liked being in control.

I wonder what it would be like to be Jamie, so perfect and poised all the time. So in control. It exhausts me just thinking about it.

"I will leave you in Beth's capable care, if that's OK," Ryan says. He's distracted and looking at his phone. "I have some things to take care of."

"Of course you do, Mr. Gentry," I say. "You've always been in demand."

Ryan chuckles. "My in-demand days were so long ago now. Bad memories and big mistakes. Actually, I'll stay out here with you two. Why not spend some quality time together?"

22

AMELIA

I notice Beth's demeanor has shifted and her arms are crossed on her chest.

"Big mistakes, Ryan?" she says. "Like Sunny?"

Ryan leans forward so their eyes meet across me. "Of course not Sunny. She was perfect."

Yes, that's what happens when you die young, I think. I'm far from perfect, of course, especially at this moment, but I look the part. I'm always dressed in the finest couture, my hair and makeup precise; my expectations of myself are as high as they are for others. When I appear, whether at a society gala or in front of my kids in our home, I am the star of the show. My show. Always. Even sitting here on the pickleball court, I look like a million bucks.

I don't know what the tension is between these two, but this should all be about me. My cheek stings. Stupid Brett. And my eyebrow is tender. For a moment I wonder if he hit the ball at me on purpose, but then I realize he's smitten with me. I'm the one who is getting over him. Quickly.

I'd better not have a bruise.

"Can you get me some water?" I ask Beth. Giving her something to do will force her to stop hovering over me. Usually I like the attention, of course. But it's only Beth, so I turn off my charm.

"Sure, of course," Beth says, standing up.

"I've got an extra Gatorade over there," Ryan says, pointing to a cooler near the court. "I think all the waters are gone."

"Um, no, I don't need all those calories," I say but soften my tone. It's Ryan and he's cute. "But thank you."

"I'll go get you water from inside," Beth says.

"Could you bring that article you said you found too?" Ryan says. "I don't know what it was doing in your room."

"Sure, yes, I'll grab both," Beth says and hurries away.

I watch her until I lose sight of her in the lush grounds. Now that she's gone, maybe I can find out what is going on between Roxy and her husband.

I sit on the court next to Ryan, just the two of us, hidden from the sun by the palm tree fronds.

"I think your face is going to be fine," Ryan says.

"Fine?" I say. Is that the best he can do?

"Beautiful, as always," he assures me. That's more like it.

"Good man," I say.

"Jamie will have the final say, of course," he says.

"Yes, it's always nice to have a doctor in the house." I pause to choose my next words carefully. "But speaking of houses and the people inside them, what's up with you and Roxy?" I say. "You guys seem a little out of sync, to put it mildly."

"What? No, we're fine," he says.

"Come on. I've been watching you two and things don't look fine," I say. "You can tell me anything."

"Drop it, Amelia," he says. And smiles. "You always did like to stir up trouble, find problems that weren't there."

"I'm not talking about me right now," I say and flash him a smile back. It hurts my cheek. "It's so obvious, I mean, especially for all of us who have known you for so long."

"Oh, really? Is that the sorority gossip du jour?" he asks. His face has tensed, and his eyes are dark. It's almost like he's a different Ryan, unrecognizable. "I hate gossip, Amelia. I always have, as you know, so you can mind your own business and enjoy our over-the-top hospitality, OK?"

I smile, remembering those same words coming out of his mouth. We were standing in the backyard of the sorority house at a fall party senior year when he and Sunny, hand in hand, confronted me.

"What the hell were you thinking?" Ryan had said, leaning forward into my space.

I had been having a lovely evening at our party with several different, suitable hookups for later. The guy I had been flirting with scurried away when he heard Ryan's tone.

"I *was* thinking about asking Mr. Brown-Eyed Hottie if

he wanted to accompany me to my room, but thanks to your interruption, I guess that's not happening now," I said, annoyed. I smoothed my party dress and looked around, anxious to get back to the boy he scared away.

"You know exactly what we're talking about, Amelia, so please don't try to play dumb. You told a whole group of Kappas that I was pregnant and had an abortion," Sunny whispered while shaking her head, her long blond hair spilling over her shoulders, her green dress a perfect match to her eyes. She was annoyingly pretty even when she was angry.

"No, I didn't," I said. "But that is what everyone has heard. I mean if I've heard it, I'm sure all of them have too. It's spread across campus." I open my arms wide, indicating our entire chapter and their guests.

"You know that isn't true," Sunny said. "Why would you repeat such a thing? You're my friend. You could've asked me."

"And even if you thought it was true," Ryan said, "you could have shut down the whispers and told people it's none of their business—which it isn't. Instead, you fed the rumor mill for, what, your own amusement? What the hell, Amelia? I hate gossip, and I hate gossipers," he said. He wrapped his arm protectively around Sunny. They looked irritatingly perfect together, what today's generation would call #CoupleGoals.

"Maybe you're right. I could have stood up for you, but I don't know, I didn't start it," I said. "I wouldn't start a rumor like that." Well, I would and I could, but this particular time, I didn't.

Ryan and Sunny stared at me, I guess trying to decide

whether I was telling the truth. The silence was awkward, and I had a party to get back to.

"Ryan, she said she didn't do it," Sunny said, standing up for me. "Don't worry. We don't hate you."

Oh goody. Miss Sunshine and her man were still my friends. I didn't say another word, simply turned and walked away. But I always remembered that look on Ryan's face. It's the same look he has right now. I decide to appease him. I mean, I don't want the man to have a stroke or anything.

"I didn't mean to upset you. I was only asking a question. What with the house renovations and the wedding planning, I'm sure you and Roxy have so much going on that it's stressful," I say and pat his hand. "You just relax and enjoy yourself. Roxy will take care of everything, like she always does. And clearly I misread the relationship vibe. I'm sure all is dandy and nothing is going on."

Ryan suddenly finds something interesting to stare at on the other side of the court. Finally, he turns to me. "You're right, Amelia, there's absolutely nothing going on between Roxy and me."

Well, you know I don't believe that answer. I see more than they give me credit for, as usual. But it sort of makes me happy that there's trouble in paradise. It really does.

23

BETH

After the drama of Amelia's injury—and it was all drama, no trauma, as far as I could see—it was nice to watch Jamie in action with her doctor bag and supplies, taking charge. She moved Amelia to a lounge chair in the garden before checking her injury, which seems to simply require an ice pack. Brett, the poor sport, also returned from his room and offered Amelia pills, which she declined. Jamie seemed furious he was intruding on her care.

Ryan and I decided we didn't need to stick around, and I was more than happy to get back out on the pickleball court. The second match went even better than our game against Jamie and Brett. Ryan and I trounced Roxy and Greer, who came over to the courts to watch and ended up playing. I cannot stop smiling as we sit down for a late lunch in the oversized dining room. Outside the windows a trellis adorned with pink bougainvillea vines rustles in the breeze.

Everything about this place is perfect except one small thing: When I went to find the newspaper from the day Sunny died, it was gone. And now, I'm beginning to think it was never there at all. From the look on Ryan's face when I told him, I could tell he thought I was making the whole thing up. I wasn't. I wouldn't. Would I?

"Are you sure the newspaper was really there?" he'd asked as we walked to the pickleball court.

"It was," I said. But I was beginning to have my doubts.

"Well, if it or anything else like that turns up, please let me know," Ryan said.

"The photo of the young woman, in the hallway outside my room—did you realize the model looks like Sunny?" I asked.

"I don't know what you're talking about," Ryan said, giving me a look like I'm losing it. "Look, Roxy and Greer are ready to play. Get your game face on."

I did, and we won big. Now, as I walk into the gorgeous dining room, I remind myself I'm Roxy's guest. I should have an attitude of gratitude, as they say. But I can't help myself. It's so nice to see the high and mighty Roxy put in her place for once. She is a sore loser, although not as violent as Brett was when we beat him. Ryan pulls my chair out for me.

"Here you go, partner," he says as I sit. I know I'm grinning from ear to ear. I'm also Ryan's guest, not just Roxy's, and he seems to appreciate my company much more than his wife does.

Roxy gives me a sharp look. "So did I tell you all about the fabulous bachelorette party I've been planning for Celeste, with her input of course?"

Celeste and I lock eyes, and she mouths "don't worry" and shakes her head. I try not to let Roxy get to me, but as usual, she does. This is why I couldn't stand her in college. Roxy always loved putting me in my place, letting everyone know I was the scholarship student, the poor one, as often as she could. And now she has the nerve to do it in front of my own daughter.

As Roxy rattles on and on about her fabulous plans for Celeste and her bridesmaids, I glance through the window of the dining room. The sunshine we'd enjoyed earlier is gone, replaced by gray skies and—if the furiously swaying palm trees and the flying pink petals of the bougainvillea are any indication—gusty winds. It looks like we'll be staying inside for the rest of the afternoon. I feel a sense of relief.

Truth is, the more time I spent playing pickleball, and I really enjoyed myself, the more I'd found my eyes drawn to the swimming pool in the distance. The rectangular pool with decorative tile is a nod to the art deco architecture and design that was prevalent in the 1920s in Palm Springs. And it's too much like the pool where Sunny died. A chill runs down my back thinking about it.

A thick fog comes out of nowhere as I watch out the window and the tennis court fades from view. The vibrant colors of the flowers and greenery are becoming muted, as if a hazy curtain has dropped over the yard. The longer I watch, the darker it gets outside, and I am not sure if it's fog or something else I'm seeing. There's a smell in the air now, of earth and dryness.

"Hey, you guys, look outside," I say. "What is happening?"

"It looks like a dust storm," Ryan says. He stands and walks to the window. "Do you hear that? The howling is the wind."

Beside me, Brett is making a strange sound. He seems to be struggling to catch his breath. He must be having some sort of panic attack. Maybe he's afraid of storms?

"Brett, are you OK?" I ask.

"I'm fine. Need some air," he says. He stumbles to the door leading outside from the dining room, pushes it open, and hurries outside.

"Brett, you really shouldn't go out there," Ryan calls. But Brett either doesn't hear him or chooses to ignore him. Ryan swears under his breath. "I'll go get him."

"Ryan, wait, you need a face mask, and one for Brett. One minute," Roxy says and hurries out of the room.

We all watch as Brett stumbles around outside, but it's surreal. The thick dust makes it hard to see anything clearly, even a large man like Brett. The formerly bright landscaping has become ghostly silhouettes. And then, as we all watch from the window, Brett disappears, obscured by the swirling dust.

"Somebody go get him! We can't just stand here," Amelia says, rushing to the door, watching anxiously as we all are. "I'm not going out there."

Roxy returns to the room. "I couldn't find masks."

"I'll get him. Everyone stay inside; it's dangerous out there," Ryan says and disappears into the storm.

It's not more than five minutes later, as we all stand looking out the windows, hoping to see them coming back inside, that we hear Ryan yell, "Help! Jamie! Help!"

Jamie looks at me and says, "Come with me, Beth. Greer, let's go."

"Mom, don't go out there," Celeste says.

"I'll stay with you," Zach says, wrapping his arm around her.

"I'll be right back," I say. I grab the napkin from the table and cover my nose and mouth and follow Jamie and Greer into the chaos. The air is thick and hot, and the dust feels like soot. Tiny pieces of gravel sting my exposed skin.

None of us can see farther than our outstretched hands. We walk carefully, and slowly. Until Ryan yells again, over the storm: "Come to the pool!"

Before I know it, we've reached the swimming pool. And there's a body floating in it.

I hear myself screaming as I see Jamie jumping into the water and, with Ryan and Greer's help, dragging a limp Brett to the side. We all help pull him out of the pool and watch helplessly as Jamie performs CPR. She works on him for what seems like hours; I don't know how long we all stand there, hoping, watching in terror.

And the flashbacks come before I can stop them, of Sunny, floating, dead in the pool, the pool that looked so much like this one. Her green shirt. Her ponytail. Her tennis necklace. All of them flash through my mind. I cough and rub my eyes. The dust is everywhere, in my mouth, my eyes, my nose. We huddle together around Jamie and Brett, trying to shield her, them, from the storm.

Brett isn't moving, hasn't moved since they pulled him out of the water. Amelia has joined us outside, standing silently, watching. None of us speak.

And the reality begins to sink in. Despite Jamie's best efforts at reviving him, we eventually have to face the truth.

Jamie stops CPR, leans back, and shakes her head.

"I did all I could," she says, her face covered in dust and mud, her eyes exhausted. "But I'm afraid Brett is dead."

24

AMELIA

People swirl around me in the kitchen, yelling, wet, crazed, in shock. It's a relief to be back inside the house, but I'm still disoriented from being out in the storm. The air is dirt, and the floor beneath my feet feels like it's swaying slightly, back and forth. It's pandemonium, and yet, I feel calm. It's strange. I pinch my own arm. Pat my cheek and eye socket where the pickleball hit me. I don't feel anything. Not pain, not sorrow or grief.

Once I got over the shock of seeing Brett in the pool, face down, and then waterlogged and lifeless on the deck, the only emotion I've managed to feel is indifference. It's not like I'd known Brett all that well, to be fair. We'd hooked up a few times, sure, and the sex was great, but I certainly hadn't been in love with him. That much is clear. He was annoying and became even more so each minute of this weekend.

Why did he turn out to be such a flirt, such an ass, and such a bad sport? Who knows. And now, everyone is focusing on his death, trying to figure out what to do, and that means I must postpone the critical conversation I was planning to have with Roxy this afternoon. We have business to discuss, and now she, like everyone else, is completely distracted.

Despite the fact he's now dead, I'm angry at him still. This is all Brett's fault. In a short amount of time this weekend, he morphed from being a fun date into a show-off flirt. He couldn't focus on me, the most gorgeous single woman in the house. No, that wasn't enough for him. He decided it would be much more fun if he paid attention to Beth and Jamie, who has a husband who is always around her. I mean, like why flirt with Jamie? It was so strange. And then that whole pickleball situation. Part of me wonders if he hit me in the face on purpose, hoping to knock me out or get me out of the way. I guess I'll never really know what he was up to this weekend. But one thing is for certain—whatever he was up to, he won't be up to it anymore.

I watch with mild interest as Ryan, Greer, and Zach carefully carry Brett's body past me, heading to the far reaches of the house, no doubt. Outside, the haboob, as we have learned the dust storm is called, is still a menace, turning daytime into night. Hopefully, the storm will pass soon, because the emergency operator indicated they would not send a squad to collect an already dead person in this sort of weather. Brett, and the rest of us, must wait for better skies.

I wonder if he will begin to smell as he decomposes. A chill runs down my spine at that, and I'm glad at least I feel something. Disgusted.

I peek down the hallway and see that the men have placed Brett's body on top of the piano in the living room, visible from all of the first-floor entertainment areas of the house. They walk toward me in a solemn clump, leaving Brett on the baby grand, like he's awkwardly fallen asleep there. But he hasn't. He's dead. I wonder if he has a family, parents or siblings or anybody. Someone will need to break the bad news to them.

I remember that awful day when Sunny's body was discovered. Beth had to call Sunny's mom from the lobby of the hotel while we all stood by her for moral support. It was heartbreaking, the kind of call no one ever wants to make, or receive, for that matter. It's a terrible coincidence that both Sunny and Brett died in a pool in Palm Springs. Maybe this whole town is cursed, or maybe it's us.

I stare down the hallway at Brett's body. I wonder if he's ruining the shiny finish with the pool water and whatever is leaking out of him. Disgusting. Then again, even if by some miracle the baby grand remains pristine, Roxy will probably replace it the first chance she gets. There's no way she'd be willing to have someone play a piano a dead man once rested on. I hurry away from the view down the hallway and wonder if I can make it to the pool house to change, or if the storm is still furious, a relentless swirling of dust particles. It is unsettling outside, the force of nature so powerful, so surprising. But

I'm unsettled inside, too, knowing Brett is at the end of the hall, dead. I mean, what are the chances?

So much for Roxy's big plans to create happy memories here to replace the sad ones.

25

ROXY

Nothing has gone as planned. Obviously, Brett dying in my pool was the worst possible thing. Well, one of the worst possible things. Another huge problem is that Ryan thinks we're over, which we're not, and I'll have to fix things between us. And I will. I think the stress of hosting all of these college friends here has really pushed him over the edge. They'll be gone soon, though, and we'll be fine. And then there's the haboob—I've never heard of such a thing—spitting dark sand and scary wind at us. So far this engagement weekend has been...I won't say a bust. But a challenge.

But now it is time to regain control of the weekend. I've taken a shower and changed into my dinner gown, a full-length, body-hugging silk stunner in baby blue that brings out my eyes. I look gorgeous, I do. I add some of my favorite diamond jewelry, which I brought to show off to my sisters, of course. Satisfied that I look amazing, I hurry back downstairs to find my guests. And my husband. Surely this look will help change his mind. It's his favorite color.

A shudder runs down my spine as I look down the hall to the foyer and into the living room. I know his body is on the piano, but I refuse to look at it. I'll never be able to walk past it if I see him there now I'll always see him there. I turn around and head to the kitchen, pushing the memory of this afternoon out of my mind.

We still have an engagement to celebrate. We will honor my son—and his future wife, who I've come to enjoy being around. She'll be easy to work with, malleable and compliant. A good partner for my rather dominant, strong-willed son. She was so quiet when we met the first few times, but now, I've been able to appreciate her sense of humor and her heart. She is stunning, so I'll have adorable grandchildren to spoil someday, but I'm definitely not in a hurry to be called Grandma.

I need to talk to Ryan about buying them a house near us. That's what all my friends are doing who can afford it. I mean, it's almost impossible for the kids to get a start these days. What a wedding gift that will be. Nothing but the best for my boy and his wife. I do hope she'll continue to listen to me about the wedding planning. I know what I'm doing. And her mom, well, she's over her head. Always has been, poor Beth.

When I walk into the kitchen, I see all the guests and the couple of honor, minus Brett, have gathered. It's the heart of the home and should be a relaxing space, but I can feel the tension.

Yes, someone died, tragically. But they need to refocus. They need to get cleaned up. They are a mess, and they're soiling all the new furniture. I need to remind them what this weekend is all about.

"Everyone, so glad we're all together," I say, putting on my best sorority rush face. I've still got it. Everyone knows it. I clap my hands a couple times. I need to jolt some energy into this group. They're all sitting around with sad faces, lost in thought. I really can't stand it. "Look, what happened to Brett is a tragedy. I'm not going to pretend it isn't. Everyone in this room did their best to save him, and we failed through no fault of our own. But now there is nothing more we can do to help him. And from what I saw of his lively spirit this weekend, he would want us to continue with our planned festivities for Celeste and Zach. So can we make the effort to put on our happy faces to honor his memory?"

As my gaze slides from one person to the next, I notice Amelia has dressed for dinner too. Good. I mean, if she can snap out of the misery daze, they all can. She wears a skin-tight black gown, her red hair curled and framing her neck like a lioness. There is no sign of the pickleball injury on her perfectly made-up face, and no sign of grief in her expression. She looks like nothing terrible has happened here at all. I like that. I smile at her in appreciation, but she rolls her eyes at me.

"I hope you don't mind, I grabbed one of my bags from the pool house and moved into one of the spare rooms in the main house here," Amelia says. "It's scary out there, especially now, after what happened. Nice pep talk, but you didn't even know him, Roxy."

"Sure, whatever," I say, glaring at her. "I'm being nice, respectful of the dead."

Heck, she's the one who brought him here, not me. I mean, none of them really knew Brett, and they're acting like they lost an uncle or something. I do notice the stark contrast between Amelia and me, and everyone else. I'm sure they must be as anxious to shower off the dust as I was. I still feel it in my throat, taste the earth on my tongue. A good meal will make all of us feel better.

"Look, we're all trapped here for the foreseeable future. Who knows how long this thing outside will last," I say. "And that's fine, because we've got another feast on the menu tonight. The staff should be here any moment to start getting things ready, and we have all the supplies we need to make it very special. So why don't you all go put on your party clothes and get ready to enjoy a fantastic dinner I spent weeks planning? A shower feels great, Jamie, Beth; it really does. All I need is for you all to snap out of it and go get changed. You're all covered in dust."

Ryan stands and I think for a moment he's obeying my command. My heart flutters. He'll lead the charge to the showers; he'll help me help them forget about Brett and refocus on the kids. I see him look at Zach, and they hold a look for a moment. And then Ryan takes a deep breath and turns and looks at me.

"I'm sure you think you're being helpful right now. But we are all sick of this, this Roxy Show," he says, his blue eyes flashing at me in anger.

I feel my mouth drop in shock. I'm mortified. How can he talk to me like this, in front of all of them? In front of Zach, my boy?

"I don't know what you're talking about. I'm trying to lift everyone's spirits, to celebrate the kids, to make everything perfect," I say. I pinch my hand because I feel tears welling up in my eyes. I do not want to drip water on this gorgeous gown.

"It's not perfect, Roxy. It's about as far from perfect as you can get. A man has died; we're trapped here by a dust storm that has, according to the alert on my phone, caused a thirty-car pile-up and a raging fire near the electric transponder. The haboob should be over soon, but the damage will take days, or weeks, to recover from. But you're acting as if nothing is wrong. I know I promised to behave in front of the guests, to play my role in your show, but I can't, not anymore." Ryan is shaking his head, hands on his hips. I don't like the looks of this, not at all.

He can't do this. "No, stop talking—you can't do this. Not here. Not now," I say. I reach for the kitchen counter behind me to steady myself.

Ryan sweeps his gaze around the room. "I'm sorry to make a scene in front of you all, but I don't feel comfortable lying to you any longer. Roxy and I are getting a divorce," he says.

I hear someone gasp. I suspect it was Amelia, though I cannot bring myself to meet anyone's eyes. The room has gone silent again, but this time it's because of us, our marriage, imploding in front of them.

"Ryan, please," I say. I can't stop the tears running down my cheeks.

"I'm sorry, everyone. I truly am," he says and strides out of the room.

I hold on to the counter behind me, certain if I let go, I'll slump to the floor. I do my best to maintain my bright smile because no matter what, the show must go on. Even if I am watching the life I worked so hard for unravel before my eyes.

26

AMELIA

I watch as one by one the guests make excuses to leave the kitchen. Jamie, who has been pale and withdrawn since her failed attempt to resuscitate Brett, stretches her arms in the air and stands up. Her pickleball outfit is covered in a mixture of mud and dirt, mud from the swimming pool water, dirt from the dust storm.

"I'm taking a shower and then a nap," she says and walks out of the room. I don't blame her. It looked like hard work, what she did, and all to no avail. It must be tough on doctors when their patients die. I mean, not that Brett was actually a patient of hers, but still, she was the doctor who tried to save him. And they were pickleball partners for a moment.

"I'm going to go check on the latest weather report," Greer says, following Jamie out of the room. "Maybe the phone service is better in our room."

Zach has been staring at his mom ever since Ryan left the room. I've watched as Celeste tried to console him, but he's clearly beyond angry, and beyond words. Zach doesn't bother with an excuse when he leaves the room. He simply shoots his mom a look of betrayal as he flees the room with Celeste and Beth hurrying after him.

Finally, it's only me and Roxy, Roxy still standing by the oven, me sitting at the kitchen table.

"I guess it's just us," I say. I stand and walk over to Roxy. "Are you OK? That was quite a bombshell Ryan dropped."

Roxy begins to laugh, a maniacal chuckle that gives me the chills. She points at me, a long, thin pointer finger sporting a huge diamond and sapphire cocktail ring. "Spare me your fake sympathy. I know you're only worried about yourself and your little monthly allowance. Well, you should be, because I won't be paying you a dime of hush money from now on. I'll be too busy trying to get enough money for myself, to live on, and I won't be funding your lifestyle too. It's over."

I stare at Roxy and see her clearly, the woman she actually is. The blackmail hasn't been about the money, but she clearly doesn't realize that. I have plenty, especially now. It's been about revenge. Because it's always all about her, always has been, always will be. We are all props on her stage. I remember the last night of spring break. It was before dinner and I knocked on Sunny and Ryan's hotel room door, hoping to borrow a dress to wear for dinner and to go out that evening. I hadn't brought along enough sexy, desert options, and Sunny had looked spectacular every day and night.

The door opened and it was Roxy standing there. But I'd knocked on Sunny's door.

"What are you doing here?" I asked, confused. There was no way she was there to borrow a dress like I was—Roxy would never have been caught dead in someone else's clothes. Roxy looked uncomfortable, like I'd caught her with her hand in a cookie jar.

"Get in here I need you," she said, grabbing my arm and dragging me inside and closing the door behind me.

"OK, but what's going on?" I asked. And then I found out. Something was wrong with Sunny. Her hair was a mess, and she was mumbling to herself, walking in a circle. I rushed over to her to keep her from bumping into the wall. "What's wrong with her?"

"Um," Roxy said and shrugged.

"Sunny? What's going on?" I asked but her eyes were glassy; she didn't seem to see me or hear me.

"Ryan?" Sunny says in a whisper.

"We need to get her to bed," Roxy said. "Can you help me?"

"Sure, but tell me what happened?" I said again.

"I'll tell you later. For now, let's get her settled," Roxy said.

"Sunny, let's get you to bed. Sound good?" I asked her, still holding her arm to keep her from walking into the wall.

"Find Beth," Sunny mumbled.

"You need to go to sleep, Sunny," Roxy said, grabbing her other arm. Together we positioned her next to the bed and gently pushed her down. "That's it, sleep. Everything will be OK in the morning. Promise."

"Ah, sa, boke," Sunny mumbled incoherently.

"Sunny, we can't understand you. Was it too many margaritas? What happened?" I asked but she couldn't speak any longer. Sunny's typically sparkling green eyes were dull, lifeless. Her shiny blond hair, usually falling in waves down her back, was pulled up in a messy bun. She was barely recognizable, poor thing.

"You need to take a nap, girlfriend," Roxy said.

"It's the only thing that will help," I said, although a thought did cross my mind about finding a doctor.

With both of us urging her, Sunny finally agreed to close her eyes and, hopefully, clear her head. I felt sorry for her; she was so disoriented, so out of her mind. Roxy and I sat on the bed together and watched as Sunny finally fell asleep.

"How did she get like this?" I whispered. "Should we call a doctor?"

"No, she needs to sleep it off. I'm sure it was the double margarita. Those Desert Sunrise specials are strong," Roxy said before walking across the hotel room to the dresser. I watched as she rummaged through Sunny's purse and found her phone, sending off a quick text to someone. Then she dropped the phone back in Sunny's purse, grabbed my hand, and dragged me out of the room.

"Come on, she really needs to rest," she said once we were outside the hotel room with Sunny safely tucked inside in bed.

"OK, now that she's sleeping, do you mind telling me what the hell happened to her?" I asked.

Roxy looked at me with a small smile. "I might have brought a couple of those signature margaritas to Sunny's room. I thought we'd pregame before dinner. Sunny thought it was a great idea."

"Those margaritas don't cause that kind of reaction," I said.

"No, they don't, you're right," Roxy said, tossing her head. She looked at me with a devilish grin. She was quite pleased with herself for some reason.

"OK, why are you grinning? What have you done?" I said.

"You're right. Margaritas don't do that to people, but roofies do. Did I not mention that I slipped some into her drinks? My bad. I probably forgot to tell Sunny that too. I mean, it's our last night and you know I've had a crush on Ryan since freshman year. This was the only way to get him alone, away from her. She'll be fine in the morning, and meanwhile, I have my chance at true love. I'll make him fall for me tonight."

27

AMELIA

I should have been horrified. I should have told her she'd violated every rule in the sorority's code of conduct, every rule of any society, but I wasn't, I'll admit it. I was impressed. I admired Roxy's ruthlessness. She was going after what she wanted, however low she had to stoop. And it was low, that's for sure.

"Wow," I said. "You're really vicious." I wondered if I should sneak back into Sunny's room and borrow that dress I was coveting. But, no, that would have been a little *too* much sisterly love for poor Sunny.

Roxy threaded her arm through mine. "I prefer to think of it as knowing what I want in life, and not stopping until I get it. And what I want most in life is Ryan."

That's when I finally noticed her outfit. It was a slinky, almost see-through white dress that left little to the imagination.

She was going all out for Ryan. Impressive and gutsy. If she was successful, she'd blow up everything, not just Ryan and Sunny, but this whole friend group too. Sunny was the glue who held us all together. She was the common bond. She treated everybody with kindness and gave us all second and third chances when we messed up. And, boy, did we mess up during college.

Everyone knew that Sunny was who our group revolved around, including Roxy. As much as she liked to think queen bees can have true friends, they really cannot. *We* really cannot. Sunny and Beth were the true best friends; the rest of us were happy to have someone like Sunny *like* us. Because being Sunny's sister, and friend, meant we were good, happy people. The Sunny seal of approval did all of that. Even if it was a smoke screen. I'd pushed all thoughts of Sunny's goodness out of my mind and focused on ruthless Roxy.

"Well, I'd wish you good luck, but in that dress, I don't think you'll need it." I felt a surprising pang of remorse for the likely demise of Ryan and Sunny. I always assumed they'd get married someday and pop out a bunch of genetically blessed babies. "I'll see you downstairs. I need to go back to my room and rummage for an outfit for our last night out."

"What were you doing here anyway? Why did you come to Sunny's room?" she asked.

"I was going to borrow a dress. I want to look like you, sexy, hot," I said.

"Tell you what. You can borrow something of mine, but I need to ask a favor," Roxy said.

"Sure, anything," I said, beyond excited to get a Roxy dress to wear.

"I need you to distract Beth. Take her out with you tonight. I need Ryan's full attention, and I know she watches him like a hawk, for Sunny," Roxy said. "I don't want poor Beth to see me plying Ryan with alcohol and taking him back to my room. That wouldn't be good."

"No, that wouldn't be," I said. "Sure, I'll drag her along to the casino with me. I met a couple of hot guys at the pool, and we are meeting at nine tonight. I'll get her playing blackjack or something and the time will fly. I don't think the guys I met would go for someone like Beth, though. I mean, why would they go for plain, conservative Beth when I'm, well, me, especially in your dress."

"OK, how you do it doesn't matter. Just keep her occupied however you can," she said.

"Deal," I said. And with that, I got a sexy dress to wear for the night, and Roxy thought she would get what she'd always wanted. And it turns out she did. Until now.

Now, Ryan's leaving her. I stare at Roxy, mascara stains on her cheeks, anger all over her face. But I can't have any more sympathy. She's slipping out of my grip. I cannot allow it.

"Roxy, I can't believe you think you can cut me off after what I did for you," I say. "You know, I could still tell Ryan the truth. I'm sure he'd love to hear it at this point. He's already so angry with you, it seems." I push my hair back from my face. When I'm mad I hate the feel of hair on my skin. And I'm mad, and maybe a little desperate.

"He wouldn't believe you," Roxy says, forcing a fake smile on her face. "He's not angry, he's confused. It's a lot, having us all back together. It's conjuring up bad things; it's, well, it was a terrible idea to bring everyone here. I should never have brought us all together again, not here, not anywhere."

"It is all your fault. You started everything—not just this weekend, but all those years ago. What would Ryan think if I happened to let slip the real reason his poor roofied girlfriend was stumbling around by the pool in the middle of the night?" I say. I stare into her cold blue eyes.

"You wouldn't dare," she says.

"Sunny was probably trying to get help, poor thing, and was too out of it to know where she was going, or what she was doing. Because of you," I say. "Because you drugged her."

Roxy laughs. "You know what would make Ryan furious? All that money down the drain. What do you think Ryan will do when he finds out how much of *his* money you've blackmailed out of me over the years?"

"I've done nothing compared to you. Everyone here would agree," I say. And it's true. She's a monster. I'm just greedy. There's a difference, I assure you.

Roxy stares at me as if sizing me up. Maybe she'd forgotten what a competitor looks like, what an equal can do to you if you cross her. We both had almost equal power in the social sphere in college. Even though she was sorority president, I was the rich girl everyone wanted to be around. Even. It's likely time for her to also realize that these days I'm winning, by far. I'm a wealthy socialite, albeit with a dead husband who will need to be replaced, and she's soon to be a lowly divorcée living alone in her big house in Newport Beach. Oh my, we could be competitors once again, on the hunt for an eligible wealthy bachelor. Ugh.

She bites her lip and regains her composure.

"Extortion is a crime, too, Amelia, darling," Roxy says, her blue eyes flashing with hatred and something else. A warning. She starts to walk out of the kitchen and then turns around. "You might want to think about that before you say a word to Ryan or anyone about any of this."

28

BETH

Zach sits on the foot of the bed, and Celeste sits next to him. I'm staring at the photo framed above the fireplace. It's black and white, like the one in my room, but this one is of a young woman with long blond hair, sitting by the pool. *Unidentified guest enjoying the pool*, reads the caption below it. I force myself to look away. It's not Sunny; it's not her, I tell myself.

"My mom does this to everyone. I'm surprised my dad survived with her this long. She's so infuriating, and controlling, and unbearable. Emasculating too," Zach says. He stands and starts pacing again, running his hand through his dark hair. "I don't get how you guys were friends with her, I really don't. I mean, I live in Chicago because I don't want to live near her. My poor dad."

"Honey, it's all going to work out," Celeste says, although she doesn't look that sure. "We'll get through the wedding and then we'll make our lives in Chicago."

She looks at me, and so I don't say anything. I don't want her to make a life in Chicago, and she knows it. I need her back in Southern California. Back home. Near me.

"Maybe we could ship Roxy to Chicago, and you guys can come back home," I say. I'm trying to lighten the mood. Zach doesn't look at me. I'm getting the feeling he doesn't take advice from women, at least not from me.

"Mom," Celeste says, "I can handle this."

I am not sure she can. I look at the wall with the dent in it the size of Zach's shoe.

"I'm kidding about sending Roxy to Chicago. Sort of," I say. "Look, I'm going to go back to my room, get cleaned up for dinner. I suggest you guys do the same. It will make you feel better to get all the dust off. And maybe your parents will have reached an agreement by then, and things will be more cordial." I can only hope I'm telling the truth. It looks like we'll all be trapped here together, at least until the storm passes. I don't have it in me to weather a storm of Roxy's emotions at the same time, so I hope they will all settle down and be civil.

"What my parents need to do is agree to never speak to each other again," Zach says. He's clenching and unclenching his fists as he walks. "Especially my mom. I'm so glad you aren't anything like her, Celeste."

There's nobody quite like Roxy, fortunately. "I'm sorry. This is the toughest on kids, no matter their age," I say. "OK, I'll be right down the hall and up the stairs if you need me. Take some deep breaths. Both of you."

Back in my bedroom, I take a long shower and give myself a chance to pause and think.

Zach's one-sided blame isn't right. Celeste and I both told him that all relationships involve two people, and to solely blame his mother for his father's unhappiness was unfair, even if we are talking about Roxy.

For once in my life, I may actually feel a bit sorry for Roxy. Just a tiny bit. I mean, her entire life just imploded publicly in front of all her guests, her sorority sisters. Her reputation with us is everything to her; I know it is. It was heart-wrenching to watch, even though some part of me says she deserves it, deserves to be abandoned and divorced. Deserves to understand how it feels to be the single one, have everyone think there is something wrong with you because you don't have a man. In my case, I've focused my love and attention on Celeste. Nothing else mattered, and dating was simply not something I was interested in. Now, though, with a daughter living in Chicago and engaged to be married, I should consider it, I suppose. But what am I going to do? Go on one of those apps? I'd rather be single for the rest of my life.

I finally finish my shower and enjoy the plush robe and lotions provided before starting to blow-dry my hair. It's nothing like Roxy's or Amelia's long mane, but my hair does take a bit of effort. I decide to jot down some notes for when I talk with Zach again, words of wisdom about relationships and how much moms—all moms—sacrifice for their kids. I'm not sure he'll listen, ever, but I decide I'll try. I walk around the bedroom to the bedside table, looking for a pen and paper. This isn't a hotel, so I shouldn't expect it, I know. I pull open the drawer.

"Oh my God," I say as I stare at the postcard inside the drawer. The writing says, "So glad you're here! See you soon!" And the photo on the front is a woman wearing a bright green dress, her long blond hair cascading down her back. I can't see her face. Chills roll down my spine, and I slam the door closed. Is someone trying to taunt me, trying to make me see Sunny in every room, at every turn?

There's a knock on my door. I pull my robe closed and open the door to find Celeste. Her eyes are red as if she's been crying.

"Come in, come in," I say. "What's wrong, honey? I know Zach's upset, but is there something more?"

"I accidentally took a wrong turn and found myself standing next to that Brett guy. He's lying there, dead on the piano," she says, and I see she's shaking. "This whole weekend is a disaster. There's a storm of dirt and dust outside, a dead man, Zach's parents announced a divorce, there's a huge fire burning out of control and heading this way. I don't know. Maybe I'm not supposed to be getting married. What if I'm the bad luck charm?"

29

BETH

I pull my daughter into a hug. None of this is her fault.

"It's a lot to take in, everything that's happened, but you're the good in the weekend, my darling," I say. "Life always throws curveballs, and these are some big ones. It's OK to take a moment and catch your breath." I know I can't push her too hard to reexamine her relationship with Zach, but maybe they're moving too fast. And it's not just because he's Roxy's son.

"I do love him, but I don't want him to all of a sudden decide to leave me, like his dad did to his poor mom," Celeste says. She takes my hands in hers, and we look each other in the eye. "Like what my dad did to you."

"Seriously, honey, in my case it was good riddance. Amelia was right about that guy, unfortunately, but at least you got his good looks," I say. I glance out the window and notice the storm's dying down, the dust caught in the soft rays of the setting sun, creating a surreal spectacle. The dust has been replaced by smoke, though, and I wonder how close the fire is coming to us. I'm sure we'll receive a warning if we need to evacuate. I'm reminded of the transient nature of moments like this, like the particles dancing in the desert wind. The symbolism is not lost on me. Just as the storm has transformed the landscape outside, my daughter's engagement marks a significant shift in the landscape of her life. And mine. I squeeze her hand.

"I'm sorry about your dad," I say. "I know that's a void in your life. One I've tried my best to fill."

"I know, Mom. And you did. I didn't need him in my life, but you're right, unfortunately I do look a lot like him. But most importantly, I have your dimple," she says.

"The crowning glory of your gorgeousness," I say, smiling.

"You don't think I'm making a mistake with Zach, do you? Getting married to him? I mean, I think he's great, I love him, but what if he isn't?" she says.

"Oh, honey, I know this is a big decision, and you guys have moved very fast. You're in love with Zach, and I've seen how much he cares about you," I say carefully. "All marriages are, at some level, a leap of faith. No one totally knows the other person, what's in their heart, what they are capable of, or who they will become. But that's why it will be a journey, hopefully filled with more good than bad. And when the bad does come, as it will, you handle it together and grow stronger."

She walks to the window, lost in thought. I'm certain doubts have crept in, and it's normal to get the wedding jitters. But most young people don't witness the last gasp of a marriage on their engagement weekend, I suppose.

And the last gasp of a weekend guest, for that matter too.

Celeste turns around and smiles. "You're right. I love Zach and he loves me and that's what matters."

"It does," I agree. Love matters, and so do patience and a sprinkle of good luck. Oh, and money. Money helps a lot, and at least there will be plenty of that for the newlyweds.

"Mom, do you know what's happening tonight? Are we still having the fancy dinner?" Celeste asks. "I feel so terrible for Roxy. She must be devastated."

"Roxy will want to go on with the show. She's been planning it for months, and it's her big night," I say. "Why don't you go get dressed and we'll head down early? Offer to help? That'll give Zach some time alone to think."

"Yes, we should. You're so great, Mom, you know that?" she says.

"Back atcha, kid," I say. "I'll meet you downstairs in half an hour. And Celeste, stay away from the living room and foyer. I'll find something to cover Brett—to cover the body—but stay away."

"Good idea, and thanks, Mom," she says, and she's gone.

I make quick time of changing into my formal gown, attire specified in the Details section of the weekend's program. Tonight, I'm wearing a navy silk dress with crystal straps. I picked it because it makes me appear to be wearing jewelry like Amelia and Roxy when I don't have any real pieces like they've had on display this weekend. I know I can't keep up with them, but I did want to add a little sparkle tonight. I glance at the bedside table and think about the postcard inside. I don't know who put it there, or why. I check. The other bedside drawer is empty.

This whole trip has made me feel unsettled, and I hope I'm not imagining things that aren't there. I think about bringing the postcard to dinner with me. I decide against it. The rest of them will think I'm going mad. Of course it's not Sunny on the postcard. It couldn't be. Sunny couldn't be glad I'm here. She died long ago. I shake my head.

I walk out of my room and make a quick search for a linen closet, finding one down the hall. I grab the plainest-looking sheet I can find amid the fancy dream linens and hurry to the living room, a spectacular room off the front foyer. As I step through the ornate double doors, I'm suddenly in a space that blends art deco design elements with the distinctive Spanish Colonial influences of the area. The floor is covered in intricately patterned tiles, while a grand, handwoven Persian rug anchors the room with its vibrant colors and intricate motifs. Large windows frame the outdoors, adorned with luxurious drapes. The centerpiece of the room is a sumptuous seating arrangement, with two plush, velvet-upholstered sofas and armchairs with carved wood frames adorned with gold leaf. The entire room is a harmonious blend of jewel tones, reflecting the exuberance of the roaring twenties. The room is punctuated with brass table lamps, crystal decanters resting on polished mahogany side tables, and everything is illuminated by a grand chandelier with cascading crystals. It's all so glamorous and sophisticated, truly a work of art. The piano is in front of me, the centerpiece of this section of the first floor.

The only thing out of place in this room is Brett, whose body is sprawled on top of the piano. I don't look at his face as I cover him with the sheet. I wrap myself in a hug and hurry out of the glorious space, unsettled by the juxtaposition of grand life and tragic, sudden death.

I can't believe everything that has happened in the last twenty-four hours. Arriving here and discovering Ryan and Roxy's Palm Springs home is a near replica of the Desert Sunrise, then a sandstorm hits, followed by Brett's shocking death. Ryan's divorce bombshell capped off the afternoon. It's a lot to take in, as I told Celeste. Hardest of all, though, are the visions of Sunny flooding my mind, attempting to drown me in memories.

30

BETH

It's like being back here, back in this nearly identical setting in the desert, has opened the floodgates, and I cannot seem to close them. And now I'm beginning to see her here at Gentry House, little signs of her everywhere, in paintings and glimpses, hints and nightmares. I remember like it was yesterday the mischief in Sunny's smile when she told me we were going to a fancy hotel for spring break.

"Beth, look at this place," Sunny had said, pointing to the website for the Desert Sunrise and scrolling through photos of the property. Her hair was up in a high ponytail, and her green eyes sparkled with excitement. I wanted to be as excited as she was, and I tried to smile. "Look at the pool. We are going to get so tan."

"It looks amazing, and expensive," I'd answered. Sunny knew I couldn't afford a trip for spring break, certainly not to a luxury hotel in the desert. The SCU campus was only a two-hour drive away. "You guys will have a great time."

"You mean *we* will have a great time. You and me. It's already booked. My treat! You'll have your own room, and I'll share with Ryan, if he behaves himself," Sunny said.

"Sounds too good to be true. But I can't have you pay my way," I said. A weeklong trip, even though we could drive to the desert from campus, would be too much for my limited budget.

Sunny grinned and jumped out of her chair, wrapping me in a big hug. "Well, actually it's Theta Gamma Mu's treat. I borrowed from the sorority's party fund to pay your way. Spring break is one big party, after all, and you're not missing it. So many fraternity and sorority seniors are booking hotels out there. It's going to be one huge party."

"What? Really? Can you do that?" I asked. I knew my best friend would do anything for me, but I didn't want her to get into trouble. "I think it's too much."

I looked around the room we'd shared for the past two years, walls covered with boy band posters and fairy lights. Our twin beds had matching purple spreads and an array of throw pillows we'd picked up along the way. Our desks were side by side, messy with textbooks and candy wrappers, and each of us had a bulletin board above our desks with cherished mementos pinned to it Polaroid snapshots captured spontaneous moments that turned into memories. Our clothes hung on rolling racks—the room didn't have its own closet, but we didn't care. The racks showcased our low-rise jeans, velour tracksuits, and our sorority garb.

I was going to miss this room. I was going to miss Sunny when we graduated. We'd been together since move-in day freshman year when we discovered we were roommates. I wanted to be with her on spring break; I wanted more memories together. I looked at her and shook my head.

"You can't, Sunny," I said. I put my hands on my hips and shook my head again.

"Oh, but I can," she said with a grin. "There's an upside to being the chapter's treasurer and having sole access to our bank account. It's a justifiable expense. Think of how much work you put into our charity fundraiser. This will be the sorority's little way of saying thanks."

I was so excited I couldn't think of anything to say except, "I'm speechless."

"You work so hard, Beth. School, your part-time job, and being the philanthropy chair for the chapter, you need to have some fun. And we will," Sunny said, sitting down at her desk.

I drew in a breath, feeling the grin take over my face. "In that case, I accept. Thank you so much."

"Totally my pleasure. It's nice to use my treasurer powers for good. Trust me, there are other Theta Gams who make this job a lot less fun."

"Really? Like who?" I'd asked, intrigued and sitting back down beside her at our desks.

"Well, I can't divulge names, but I can tell you that I've had to threaten one member who is falling far behind on monthly dues, and another who I caught stealing money to buy drugs," she said with a frown. "It's tough. That's why providing you with the ability to join the chapter on spring break feels right; it *is* right. I'm not stealing money for nefarious purposes. I'm helping a sister. And that's what sororities are supposed to be about."

"You're the best. And, wow, I had no idea you've been dealing with all of this," I said, truly shocked. She'd never mentioned any of this to me before. As far as I could tell, all my fellow Theta Gams had picture-perfect lives. But maybe I hadn't been looking closely enough. "I'm sorry. Tell me who they are. Maybe I can help you?"

Sunny looked up from her laptop, considering, perhaps, revealing the identities of the rotten sisters.

"I can't. I wish I could because you'd never guess, but I can't," she said and turned back to her homework.

I never did find out who Sunny was referring to that day. It could have been anyone. Now I'm standing in the formal living room, my back to the dead body, when I feel a hand on my elbow and startle. I hadn't heard anyone walk into the room.

"God, you scared me," I say to Ryan, studying him while I wait for my racing heart to calm. "Don't you look handsome." His dark blue, perfectly tailored suit was more than handsome and made his eyes reflect an even darker blue.

"Thanks. And you look beautiful. You've always been beautiful, and you don't even know it," he says with a smile on his face that doesn't reach those blue eyes. He touches my shoulder. "I'm sorry for my outburst earlier. It was unacceptable. Roxy has pushed me too far, and I exploded."

"Please don't apologize to me; I think Roxy is the one who deserves that," I say. "Shall we go check on the dinner arrangements? I didn't want to leave it all up to Roxy, after everything that's happened."

"Don't worry. Roxy has an entire team at her disposal. Fortunately, they are housed in another wing of the property, out of sight but close enough to still make it here during the storm, with face coverings, of course," Ryan says. "It's a large estate, with plenty of places to hide staff, and other things."

"I wondered how everything would get done in this storm," I say. That explains it. Staff a minute away. We've stopped walking and are in the front entryway, another déjà vu part of the house that is eerily like the lobby of the Desert Sunrise. Sunny's smile pops into my head before the memory melds into a vision of her floating face down in the pool.

Stop it, I tell myself.

"Are you feeling all right?" Ryan asks.

My face must be giving my thoughts away. I paste on a smile. "Of course. How could I not be. We're all together to celebrate our children."

Ryan chuckles. "Is that really why we're here? Do you believe that?"

31

BETH

I look at Ryan, trying to understand his cryptic comments. "You know, I wish you had called me and told me what to expect at this place. It's so unsettling, at least at first. Maybe it still is for you? Or maybe now that it's your home, you're past that, past what happened to Sunny."

"I'll never get over what happened to Sunny. The guilt. It's crushing, isn't it?" he says. "None of us were there for her. I should have been there for her."

I swallow and stare into his eyes. "I agree. But it's no one's fault, just a tragic accident."

"Right," Ryan says. He begins to walk down the hall. "Let's go get a drink. Everything is better with a cocktail in your hand."

That's when I remember what I found. "Wait," I say, touching his arm. He stops walking and faces me. "I found a postcard in my bedroom. It's upsetting. Did you put it there?"

"What? Of course not. What kind of postcard?" he asks. I

note the darkness in his eyes, the way his jaw is clenched. He's angry I'm accusing him of something.

"It's a photo of a woman in a green dress who looks like Sunny," I say.

"I didn't put that in your room. Why would I?" he says.

"I don't know, but it really scared me," I say.

Ryan looks into my eyes, lost in thought himself. "I'm sorry. I don't have any answers, Beth. But if it makes you feel any better, you're not the only one feeling nostalgic for the past. You know how much I loved Sunny, and then that night, and all that happened…" He closes his eyes for a moment, then opens them and regards me somberly. He reaches for my hand. "We should talk. We have things we need to say."

"There you are," Roxy says, joining us in the foyer. I don't know whether to be disappointed or relieved at her timing. She has changed into a bright lavender gown. Her makeup is reapplied, and she looks as if she doesn't have a care in the world. "Celeste and Zach are already having cocktails in the dining room area. Why don't you two join us?"

"Of course," I say and lead the way, leaving Roxy and Ryan behind. I assume they will be on their best behavior tonight, for their son's sake if nothing else. We're all trapped here together, so we might as well make the most of it.

I'm filled with pride when I see my sparkling daughter. Celeste wears a pale pink chiffon gown that makes her look like a princess, while Zach stands by her side in a dark navy suit much like his father's.

"Mom, how pretty you look," Celeste says. I kiss her cheek in thanks.

"Good evening, Ms. Harris," Zach says. "Can I get you a champagne?"

"Please, and call me Beth, remember?" I answer before taking in the room. Tonight's flowers are bright explosions of color—orange, pink, yellow, purple. The table is decorated with what must be more than one hundred candles of all different shapes and sizes, flickering and dancing among the florals. It's a stunning look. Someone has built a fire that sparks and pops in the grand fireplace. The overall feel is festive and lavish, like Roxy or, rather, like what Roxy pretends to be.

"Thank you," I say as Zach hands me a champagne flute.

"Here comes the happy couple," Zach says under his breath as his parents walk in the room. Ryan and Roxy don't appear to be speaking to each other. They're stiff and formal, and Roxy walks in front of Ryan to greet her son.

"Mom, what a night," Zach says, taking a step back from her. "I'm surprised you even showed up."

"Please, I wouldn't miss a minute of your special night. But Zach, we need to talk, maybe after dinner?" Roxy says.

"Maybe, but there's not much to talk about," Zach says.

Celeste says, "Mrs. Gentry, the room is decorated beautifully. Thank you."

"Only the best for you two," Roxy says.

Jamie and Greer and Amelia appear and are equally dressed up. We've all acquiesced to Roxy's wishes again. The gang's all here, well almost, I realize, trying not to think of Brett as we take our designated seats. This time Ryan and Roxy are at opposite ends of the table. Seems like a good plan, all things considered. I'm seated to Ryan's right, across from Amelia, who once again is dazzling in old-money pearls and diamonds and a navy silk gown that complements her red hair. The spot on her face where the pickleball struck her isn't visible; whether that's because of expertly applied makeup or the fact a bruise hasn't appeared yet, I don't know.

"How's your cheek, Amelia?" I ask, causing her to touch her face.

"Oh, I'm fine. Brett had the tougher time this afternoon, turns out," Amelia says and chuckles.

I'm not sure why she's laughing over her dead date, but then again, I can't pretend I've ever really understood Amelia. Next to me, Ryan shakes his head.

"Good evening, everyone," Roxy says, clinking her glass.

Oh no, not another speech. There cannot be anything left to say, can there? For a moment, the grand chandelier flickers, and I wonder if the power is going to go out. But then it holds, and the lights stop flickering. I meet Ryan's eye, and he looks as relieved as I feel. A power outage is the last thing we need.

32

JAMIE

I am beyond tired of all the games people are playing around here. The Roxy and Amelia show is getting old, and redundant. The truth is, I came here because I loved my time as a Theta Gamma. I loved my sisters and my chapter. I was so excited to rekindle some of that happy spirit, remember the good times.

But from the moment we arrived, and Amelia and Brett crashed the party, it's been nothing but bad behavior.

I expected more from them, from all of them, I think as I look around the table. Out of the corner of my eye I see someone moving down the hallway, a woman, wearing a long green dress. She's blond, petite.

"Sunny?" I stand up as all eyes around the table look at me.

Greer stands next to me. "Honey, what is it?"

"Nothing. I thought I saw something," I say.

"You've had a really long day," he says, helping me back into my seat. "Do you need to go back to our room?"

"No, no, I'm fine," I say and take a sip of my wine.

"Did you say Sunny?" Beth asks.

"It was my mind playing tricks on me. I thought I saw her down there, walking away," I say. "It's ridiculous."

"I saw her too," Amelia says. "I could have sworn I did. Out by the pool this morning."

"You all are letting your imaginations run wild," Roxy says, shaking her head. "Sunny isn't here. But you all are. Let's focus on the living, shall we? Let's focus on the future: Celeste and Zach."

I look at the young couple and they both are looking at me like I'm losing it. Maybe I am.

33

BETH

Jamie looks like she's seen a ghost. I wonder if I should help her, but I guess she has Greer by her side. I try to get her attention, but she's staring at something on the table. Meanwhile, Roxy, hostess with the most-est, smiles even as the lights flicker off and on. It's as if she's willing the power to stay on.

"Isn't the chandelier remarkable? Ryan curated every detail of this room, of this entire house, and he did a fabulous job," Roxy says, looking up after the flickering stopped. "So, after the stress and tension of this afternoon, I'd like to suggest that we get the weekend back on track, as much as we can."

"That's why we all came to dinner, Mom, to pretend like everything is normal," Zach says with a snarky tone. "Happy engagement weekend and all that."

"Yes, exactly," Roxy says.

"Zach, your mom has done her best, and I for one appreciate

this, or I will try to on behalf of our guests," Ryan says, his words directed at his son, hopefully trying to calm down his obvious disdain for his mother, our hostess.

"Well, I'm starving, so I'm looking forward to this meal," Amelia says. "I hope it's over the top again."

"Of course it will be. What else would you expect?" says Roxy with a smile.

"Best my money can buy, right, dear?" Ryan says.

I look at him and he shrugs. It's true, I suppose. It was his family's money that trickled down to him, and to his family. I wonder if he often reminds Roxy of that fact, even after all their years together.

"I'm glad the power is staying on, and that the storm is hopefully on its way out," Greer says. "Then we can properly deal with the uh, body, in the living room."

Jamie stares at her husband. "Can we not bring him up anymore?"

"Of course, dear, so sorry, but it wasn't your fault," he says. "You did your best to save him."

"We all saw that. You were a hero, Jamie," I say as the wait staff walk into the room with our first course.

"Kale Caesar salad with fresh edible flowers and aged parmesan," Roxy says as the plates are set in front of us. "Bon appétit!"

The salad is beautiful, an explosion of color that matches the flowers in the centerpieces. I smile at Celeste as I take a bite. Tastes as good as it looks. I notice Celeste isn't eating her salad. Poor girl. She never could eat if there was tension in the air, and there is tension everywhere in this room, in every nook and cranny.

"Enjoying your salad, Beth?" Ryan asks. His face has softened, and he looks like the Ryan I knew way back when.

"I am. It's great," I say.

"You know what's great is having you back in my life again. I hadn't realized until you arrived how much I've missed you," he says.

Across the table, Amelia is listening intently. "You two were always close in college, weren't you? Sunny's favorite people."

"Yes, we were," I say. "And it's because we both loved Sunny."

Ryan nods as he chews his salad.

"You know, I always wondered if there was more," Amelia says, slurring. "Like a little threesome or something?"

"Amelia! Stop it! Of course not," I say, glaring at her. "My daughter is sitting right there."

"Oh, I know Beth. I'm just fooling around," she says.

"Truth is, sure, I found Beth very attractive and kind," Ryan says. "She still is."

I feel my cheeks flush with the attention and the compliment from Ryan. When the *It* guy in college says he thought you were attractive, well, that's something. But none of that matters now.

"Thank you," I say, and I know my dimple is showing despite myself.

"You're welcome," Ryan says. "Your kindness reminds me of Sunny. That's why you two were best friends."

"How sweet," Amelia says.

"What's sweet?" Roxy asks from the other end of the table.

Amelia looks at Ryan and then me, and says, "Nothing. Great salad. A little on the sweet side, but still good. And with a lasting flavor. It almost reignited something for those of us seated down here."

Oh, for God's sake, Amelia.

"A love of kale," I say. "I always forget how much I love kale. Always have."

The lights flicker and dim. Someone gasps, and I think it's Jamie. She's completely on edge tonight. Thankfully, the lights hold.

"Well, certainly glad you enjoyed the salad course," Roxy says, standing up. "Before the main entrée is served, I wanted to take a moment to reflect on the great life lessons we all learned as members of Theta Gamma Mu. Lessons like always showing up for each other, like you all did tonight."

Across the table from me, Amelia snorts with laughter. Oh no. Her champagne glass is empty. Her flushed cheeks and glassy eyes suggest that it's not the first beverage she's had this evening.

No wonder Roxy said Amelia always has a drink in her hand on the society pages. I think it must be a permanent fixture.

"Oh, Roxy, please. I cannot take one more minute of this pretense, this act you're putting on. We never should have come here. I realize that now," Amelia says.

"The rest of the weekend will be perfect, I promise," Roxy says, a level of panic in her voice. "We're all here, we showed up for each other. Drop it, Amelia."

"I can't, Roxy. Showing up for each other was the lesson to be learned, I suppose," Amelia says as the lights dim and brighten. "But you didn't learn it. You still haven't and that's easy to see now. You're older; your mask is slipping. Heck, you didn't want us to show up. You wanted to outshine us, and I'm sick of it. I was during college and you're worse now," Amelia says before standing and walking over to the bar in the corner of the room, helping herself to another glass of wine.

She turns and glares at Roxy, pointing her finger at her. "We all know you've always been more interested in showing others up—as poor Sunny learned the hard way."

34

ROXY

I am beyond tired of being humiliated in my own home, during my own son's engagement weekend. My heart pounds in my chest as I realize I cannot escape what Amelia said. I feel everyone's eyes burn into me as they did earlier in the day when Ryan announced he was leaving me. Now, I see Amelia's drunken triumph, my son's confusion. And I see Ryan's dawning horror.

I should leave the table, but there's nowhere to go. I know my face is drained of color. I will try one last time to pivot the conversation. Amelia's drunk. She's not to be trusted.

"Amelia, I don't know what you're talking about. I loved Sunny. We all did. There was no showing her up, only admiring her beauty," I say, watching Ryan at the other end of the table closely. He's clasped his hands in front of him, frozen in his seat. "You're drunk. You should sit down before you fall over."

"You wish I'd fall over, don't you?" Amelia says and walks back to her seat.

I stare at her. I wish I had a way to get her out of here, out of this room, out of my life again.

"Zach, Celeste, could you please excuse us? Maybe enjoy your dinner in the kitchen," Beth says. "I'm sorry, but we need to discuss this audience-free. It's private. Could you give us the room?"

"Sure, Mom," Celeste says, standing and hurrying to Zach's side of the table, taking his hand and leading him away like a pink fairytale princess. She's starting to get on my nerves, but I'm not sure why. Maybe it's Beth, her seemingly perfect mom, always looking out for the kids. I suppose she is right. They shouldn't be in here, not if Amelia goes through with her threat.

I watch the poofy pink princess lead my son away. This isn't a fairy tale, though. It's a nightmare. And I don't know how to make it stop, how to wake up. I look around the table and sink slowly back into my seat in defeat.

"I loved Sunny," I say. "I did."

"Uh, huh, so much that you wanted her out of the way," Amelia says. "You'd better come clean. It's time."

"Would you like to explain yourself, Roxy? What did you do to Sunny?" Ryan says. He stares down the table at me with a look that I can only describe as hate. I slump a bit lower in my seat, trying to hide behind the beautiful explosion of flowers that adorn the table. I feel his stare, nonetheless.

"I didn't do anything, not on purpose," I say, although that's a lie.

"Tell us what happened," Beth says. Her innocent big eyes are driving me insane. I cannot hold this inside anymore. Everything is ruined anyway. My husband is leaving me, my college friends aren't really my friends. Nothing is real. Nobody is true. I have no choice but to answer Ryan's question, truthfully.

I deserve it, I suppose. For twenty-five years I've been carrying this burden, this secret. For twenty-five years I've paid for my sin, and not just literally in the form of Amelia's blackmail. In every part of my life, awake and asleep. I sit up tall in my seat and face my husband, and the rest of them, my sisters.

"I know you never loved me like you did Sunny," I say, meeting Ryan's eyes, "no matter how hard I tried to earn your love, and God knows, I've tried. That is the truth."

I think back to senior year, after Sunny died. I made sure Ryan had a comforting shoulder to cry on as he navigated his grief the remainder of our senior year. The night of our graduation, we hung out together, the two of us, missing Sunny. I did miss her too. Her genuine friendship. She was the only one who kept us all together, who accepted me for who I was. When her name was mentioned in a eulogy during our graduation ceremony, I broke down. We drank too much, trying to forget the pain. Ryan was so drunk and depressed that he'd succumbed to my advances that night, and we'd had sloppy, quick sex. He had forgotten to use a condom. I didn't remind him.

"I always tried to pretend that your proposal of marriage was enthusiastic, heartfelt," I say as tears roll down my cheeks. "But I know it was only because I told you I was pregnant a few weeks after graduation night. You never loved me, as much as I pretended that you did. You loved Sunny, and now you love Zach. But that's all."

Ryan stares at me across the vibrantly decorated table, the bright colors at odds with the darkness outside, the darkness of the moment, the deathly silence at the table. He doesn't offer up a word of denial.

"Roxy, would you like to come with me, take a break? I can walk you to your room," Jamie says, patting my hand. "I think we've all had about as much as we can handle for tonight."

"Oh, please, Jamie, don't tell me you're falling for those crocodile tears," Amelia says, her eyes flashing with glee. "Trust me, you won't want to escort Roxy anywhere after you hear what she did. You might as well tell them everything, Roxy. If you don't, I promise I will."

I've never hated her more than at this moment. That's why I didn't invite her here in the first place. I knew she would try to ruin everything. Her red hair is garish. She is the devil in the room. I look down at my hands clasped in my lap. I don't have a choice. Amelia has threatened to reveal everything, and I have no doubt she will. I know there is nothing I can do or say to salvage either the weekend or my marriage, so, what the hell. Why not tell the truth?

"I'm fine, Jamie. Thank you for caring about me, but Amelia's right. You won't want to be my friend after I tell you what I've done," I say. I take a deep breath and meet Ryan's eyes again. "It wasn't a coincidence that Sunny was too tired to party with us that last night of spring break. It was by design—my design. I wanted to seduce you, to get you alone for the night and show you what you'd been missing, so…I roofied Sunny."

"What the fuck?" Ryan explodes and stands up, banging the table with his fists. "You drugged her?"

"I did. Because Sunny had you, and I wanted you. I wanted to take you from her," I say. "I am what Amelia says I am. I like to show others up. Always have. Sunny had something I wanted, and I decided to take it. Take you."

"How did you do this? How could you do this?" Beth says, her voice wobbling with emotion.

"I slipped the roofies in a margarita I brought to her room under the guise of pregaming," I say. I cannot look up. I place my hands on the table in front of me, staring at my wedding ring. The ring I shouldn't have on and won't be wearing much longer. Everything in my life is about to be over. I look up, look into Ryan's eyes. "After she passed out, I texted Ryan from her phone that she was taking a nap. That was true, I suppose."

"Oh my God," Ryan says, his eyes flashing in rage. I've never seen him this angry. It's a little scary. And sadly, it's more emotion than he's ever shown in all the years of our marriage.

"And that's why Sunny died," Amelia says, holding up her hands to stop me from talking. "Let's connect the dots, shall we, Roxy? You roofie Sunny, she passes out, she wakes up sometime in the middle of the night, disoriented, alone, left the room, and wound up dead in the pool."

Ryan stands at the end of the table, hands clenched in fists.

Staring at me with all the hate in the world. "You really are a monster. You've been controlling me and ruining my life since the day Sunny died. How could you? You destroyed everything that was good. You saw it and you tried to take it, as if you could remanufacture it between you and me. But you are no Sunny, Roxy. You are the opposite of everything she was."

35

ROXY

The chandelier flickers over our heads. As the power wavers
on the brink of outage, the crystal droplets suspended from the
ornate arms of the chandelier seem to dance and shimmer. Tears
fill my eyes, fracturing the light further. He's right. I'm a monster.

I wipe at the tears spilling from my eyes and gaze at my husband. "And you want to know the worst part of it all? My plan
totally backfired. You turned me down that night even after I
did my best to seduce you. It was so pathetic."

"How did Amelia know what you did to poor Sunny?" Beth
asks. "And why haven't you told us this before, Amelia?"

Amelia shrugs and takes a sip of her drink. She smiles at me.
I hate her more than I can describe.

"Amelia came to Sunny's room. She saw Sunny stumbling
around, incoherent," I say, staring at Amelia, who is still smiling
at me.

"It was so Roxy, everything that happened, Ryan," Amelia says, standing and patting Ryan on the shoulder. "But you've realized that by now. She isn't who she seems. Roxy is ruthless. Ruthless Roxy. Ha, I love it. I wish I had come up with that little nickname sooner."

I exhale and point my finger at Amelia. "If I'm ruthless, then what does that make you? You've literally profited off Sunny's death." I meet Ryan's eyes again. "Ever since that night, I've paid her once a month to keep silent."

"Oh my God," Jamie says.

Greer is shaking his head. Beth appears to be in shock, as does Ryan. He stares at Amelia wordlessly before looking back at me.

"Wait a minute," Amelia says. "I thought you were with Ryan that night. I thought your plan worked. All these years that's what I thought."

"No, he turned me down," I say, my humiliation complete.

"Wow, poor thing. That really stinks to go to all that trouble to drug your so-called sister and then get nothing for your troubles," Amelia says. "But...if you weren't with Ryan, and he wasn't back in his room with Sunny, where were you, Ryan?"

I watch as Ryan's eyes dart to Beth, and then to me. Why hadn't I asked that question back then, or any time since? Somehow, in the humiliating aftermath of Ryan's rejection followed by the subsequent shock of Sunny's death, I'd never thought to bring it up. As the power teeters on the brink of failure, the crystal chandelier becomes a fleeting spectacle, like stars in a darkening sky.

"I lost my room key, so I crashed with some guys I met at the casino," Ryan says.

"I had your key card," I say. I may as well tell him the whole truth. I have nothing left to lose, not anymore. "I swiped it so you wouldn't be able to go back to your room and find Sunny drugged. And in my plans, you would be coming home with me."

"This is insane," Ryan says. "You are unwell, you know that?"

"No, I was in love," I say. "It was all for love."

"Love? You don't know the meaning of the word," Ryan snaps. "People don't roofie their friends out of love. They don't steal their room card out of love. They don't try to steal their friend's boyfriend out of love. That is not love."

"But I love you, I do," I say, and I know tears are streaming down my face again. "Ryan, please, forgive me."

Ryan shakes his head. "All these years, I have felt responsible too. If I'd been there, been back in our room when Sunny woke up, she'd still be alive. You're the one who made it impossible for me to check on her. Her death is your fault. You killed Sunny."

36

AMELIA

I've spent years wondering how I would feel if the truth about that night ever came out. I was certain, of course, that it would someday, because the truth always outs itself. Would I feel triumphant, because everyone would finally see Roxy for the ruthless manipulator that she was, and is? Would I feel embarrassed because I helped her with her scheme? Would I finally feel regret for my role in the events that led up to Sunny's death?

Now that it's all out on the table, I can't stop smiling. Beside me, Ryan is sitting stiffly in his chair, staring at his hands on the table. Beth has turned a ghostly shade of white. This must be so hard for her to hear, poor thing. Sunny was her only real friend in the sorority, the only one who would hang out with a scholarship student. I know I never would, never did. Well, except that fateful spring break.

A strange noise comes from the other end of the table. Greer is standing next to Jamie's chair, rubbing her arm in support. Jamie is crying. What's up with her?

"What now?" I ask, but everyone at the other end of the table ignores me.

"Where did you get the roofies to spike Sunny's drink, Roxy?" Jamie asks in a quiet, scared voice. She's shaking. Why is she shaking?

"I got them from Brett, of course," Roxy says. As if everyone should know that already.

I feel my brow arch with surprise. My mouth drops open. "Wait? My date? Dead Brett? That Brett?"

I had no idea Roxy even knew Brett back in their college days. He was a science TA when they were undergrads, so it's not like marketing-major Roxy was in any of his classes.

Roxy smiles slowly, a shadow of her normal cattiness returning before my eyes. She is full of surprises, this one.

"Your dear dead date, Brett. One and the same. He had quite the reputation on campus back in the day. Let's just say it's not a surprise that he went into the pharmaceutical industry. After all, he already had plenty of real-world experience handing out magic pills to cure whatever ailed you."

"Oh my gosh," Beth says, staring at Roxy. "Brett sold drugs in college?"

"Yep," Roxy says.

"Brett, a drug dealer?" I turn the concept over in my mind and realize I'm not actually all that surprised. But, God, it's probably a good thing the man is dead. If the press got wind of the fact that I had been boinking a former drug dealer, well, even I might not have been able to come back from that scandal. I'd never see my face on the society pages again, that's for sure.

"If you don't believe me, why don't you ask our friend Jamie here? She was one of his best customers, right, Jamie?" Roxy says and Beth gasps.

"Drugs? Jamie? No," Beth says as Jamie hangs her head.

This night keeps getting better and better. "Go on, Roxy. Don't leave us hanging."

Roxy seems happy that for once this weekend she is able to turn the glare of the spotlight on someone else. "I saw Jamie buy drugs from Brett on more than one occasion. The first time was after a football game. The crowds had all dispersed back to the frat houses to party, but I'd dropped an earring, so I was searching under the stands. That's when I saw them together. I thought it might be a little romantic tryst, but instead it was a rendezvous of a different sort."

"Can you stop now? Please," Jamie says. She looks like she's going to be sick. Above our heads the chandelier flickers again, growing dimmer.

"Roxy, stop talking, would you?" Ryan says, eyes flashing with anger.

"I agree. I think Jamie has been through enough this evening, and we've all heard enough of your lies," Greer says. His face is as pale as Jamie's. "I think we should call it a night."

"I'm not lying, Greer. And why would you leave now? I'm just getting started," Roxy says, standing and retrieving a new champagne bottle from the silver stand in the corner. She pops the cork and says, "This is getting fun. We might as well all spill our secrets. I didn't confront you back then, Jamie, because sometimes secrets are more valuable later, like now. Champagne, anyone?"

"I'll have some, of course," I say, although I can tell Roxy doesn't want to come near me, almost wrinkling her nose as she pours my glass. "You said that was the first time you saw Jamie making a drug deal. So there were other times too? I'm stunned. Perfect, proper, straight-A, legacy sorority president Jamie had a drug dealer?" In a weekend full of surprises, this might be the biggest one of all.

The whole scene is macabre and a little surreal, but I'm enjoying it thoroughly. "Do tell us more, Roxy," I say with a big smile. "Cheers!"

"No," Jamie says, standing and leaning against Greer. She's pale, and she's breathing rapidly. Her eyes are wide, and she looks afraid. Very afraid.

"Let's go to our room," Greer says. "Come on. You're in shock. And I don't blame you, your supposed sister treating you this way. It's unacceptable."

Suddenly, all of our mobile phones make a siren sound of alert:

> The storm-whipped fires are expected to take out all communications towers in the Palm Springs area in a matter of minutes. Roads are impassable

due to downed power lines and massive car pile-
ups. Driving is prohibited until further notice. Stay
off the roads and stay vigilant.

Of course, now that the storm has ended, we have the fire to deal with, and we're trapped here. With each other. I watch as Greer and Jamie stand to leave the room. Suddenly, Jamie turns back around.

"No, we can't leave now. This is my story to tell," Jamie says, shaking her head.

37

AMELIA

She meets my eyes defiantly. "The truth is I needed the drugs. I couldn't handle the pressure my parents put on me. They expected me to be pre-med like my dad, and president of the sorority like my mom and grandma. I turned to the college dealer out of desperation."

Greer now looks as shocked as the rest of us feel. "What? Jamie?"

"It started as a one-off—a little something to help me stay awake all night so I could cram for a test. And then there was another test, so I went back for more. Then I went back again looking for a little something to calm me down when I was having a panic attack about my course load." She sighs and gazes at her husband, who remains silent.

"Sunny knew the truth," Jamie continues, her voice quiet, shaky. "I'd run out of money, and between classwork and sorority duties, I didn't have time to get a job. So I started stealing from the sorority to fund my habit. Sunny was the treasurer. She figured out it was me siphoning money from the account."

Beth stands and puts her hands on her hips. "That was you? Sunny told me someone had taken money from the account, but she wouldn't tell me who. She wanted to talk to the person first, find a way to help them with whatever problem they were having."

"Yes, that's what she did. She talked to me," Jamie says. "She wasn't happy about it, but she agreed to let me go on the spring break trip, and then she was going to turn me in when we returned. I couldn't repay the fund, so that was her only choice. I would be kicked out of the sorority, disgraced. She was going to turn Brett in too."

We all exchange uneasy glances around the table.

"But she never made it back from spring break," Ryan says, standing up. "I can't be here right now." He drops his napkin and stomps out of the room.

Greer, looking as angry, stares at Jamie, shakes his head, and follows Ryan out the door.

"Well, ladies, we sure do know how to clear a room," I say and take another sip of champagne. I look across at Beth, then down the table to where Jamie stands next to Roxy. "A top-quality group of sorority sisters, that's what we are. Class acts."

"Knock it off, Amelia," Roxy says. "I for one am glad it's all come out. Secrets eat you up inside and ruin things, people, and relationships." Some color has returned to her face, so she doesn't look like the ice princess, but she still is one, inside. I smile. I love her discomfort.

"Well, I guess I agree. It's time to let it all go," I say. "Sunny's death was tragic, but it was an accident. Let the past stay in the past. Nothing will bring her back."

Jamie drops into her chair, seemingly exhausted. Maybe she needs some pills. I'm kidding. What she needs to do is get over herself.

"You know what?" Jamie says, tucking her blond bob behind her ear before looking down at the table. "I don't agree, Amelia. I can't let it all go."

"Good. You shouldn't," Roxy says. "You should come clean. Tell us everything. It must be eating you up inside, everything you've hidden. How embarrassing, really."

"Roxy, stop. I'll tell you," Jamie says in a quiet voice. Tears stream down her face. A dam has broken. "You're right. I can't keep this inside anymore."

Oh, great. Now what? This is getting good! What this group needs is more drama and dirt to be revealed.

"And I can't let it go," Jamie says. "Because Sunny's death wasn't an accident."

38

BETH

My blood has run cold and I'm shaking all over. What does Jamie mean? I look down the table at her like she's a stranger. She's tucked her hair behind her ears, and she looks fragile and afraid. I don't recognize her. Maybe all along she has been a stranger. Maybe they all have been.

I drop my head and stare at my hands. The dust particles against the windows of the dining room have diminished, leaving in their wake a smell of fire. Despite the assurances we are miles from the actual fire line, it's an edgy quiet that has engulfed us. It was almost better when the relentless drone of the storm outside kept us company. Now it's just us, the sorority sisters, here in the dining room reliving a nightmare that happened so long ago.

We are all, I suppose, primal forces of nature in our own right. Sunny's smile pops into my head, that delighted grin as she was talking me into accepting the free trip. The spring break trip she never came home from. She never left Palm Springs. I have my own side of the story to tell, of course, but first, I need to find out what Jamie did to Sunny.

Even though I don't want to know the answer, I must hear it. I look up at Jamie.

"What happened that night at the pool, Jamie?" I ask. The room is silent and still except for the flickering candles on the table, the acrid smell of ash outside.

"It was our last night of spring break, and I couldn't sleep. I knew Sunny was planning to turn me in as soon as we got home. I was terrified," Jamie says in a quiet voice. She wrings her hands together.

"Of course you were scared; anyone would be," Amelia says. "Sunny was a fierce one when she set her mind on something. Very black and white."

Jamie nods. "I knew Sunny would tell my parents about the drugs and report Brett to the dean," Jamie says.

"Because it was the right thing to do," I say, defending my best friend. Sunny was a light, a force for good in the world, and she was right to turn them in. But she never had a chance.

"Maybe, but I couldn't allow her to tell on me. Everything I'd worked so hard for all my life would be ruined," Jamie says, her voice stronger. "I spent the entire trip trying to figure out a way to talk her out of it, to make her see what it would do to me and my future if she told anyone about the drugs or the stealing. But it was our last night of spring break, and I still hadn't made any headway. I thought I'd have a chance to corner Sunny before dinner and beg her one last time to reconsider, but she never showed up at the restaurant. I guess we know why now," she adds, gesturing in Roxy's direction.

A chill rolls down my spine, as outside, a swaying tree creaks in the wind.

"I was so frustrated, restless. I gave up trying to sleep around three in the morning and decided I'd take a walk outside to see if I could clear my head," she says. "I ended up by the pool. I was going to sit in a lounge chair, and I don't know, look at the stars, enjoy my last evening of freedom, and not think about my ruined future."

Something slams into the window, a piece of debris that broke loose due to the wind during the storm, and Roxy lets out a yelp. "This night is going to be the end of us."

Dramatic as always. Then again, today has been a dramatic day. I turn my attention back to Jamie.

"You walked to the pool. And you saw Sunny," I say, another chill rolling down my spine.

"I saw something, someone, floating in the water," Jamie says, her voice little more than a whisper now. "As I got closer to the pool, I realized it was Sunny. I recognized her favorite pony-tail holder when it sparkled in the moonlight, and her diamond tennis necklace twinkled at the back of her neck. I went into shock, I think."

All of us fall silent, imagining the scene, the horror of it all.

"What did you do, Jamie?" Amelia slurs. "Did you help her?"

"I don't know how long she was in the water before I got there, but I think, *I think* she was still alive," Jamie says. Her blue eyes are wide with fright, with the still-vivid memory. "I thought I saw her hand twitching, but it could have been my imagination. I'm sure it was my imagination."

"Oh my God," I say, clutching my throat as if I were the one who was drowning. I find myself gasping for breath, my throat tight, restricting.

"What did you do?" Roxy says, her eyes as wide as Jamie's.

"I swear I started to dive in, to save her I swear I was going to. But something stopped me. There was this voice in my head whispering that saving her would ruin me," Jamie says. The windows of the dining room rattle with another wind gust.

We all stare at Jamie, the admission soaking into our souls, our hearts. Mine is breaking again for Sunny. My beautiful friend deserved to be saved.

"So you did nothing? You let her drown?" I say, shaking all over. "You're a doctor, you were pre-med. You have a duty to help."

"Wow, Jamie," Amelia says as she walks drunkenly over to the cooler and pours herself another glass of wine. "That's kind of diabolical. I didn't think you had it in you."

Jamie stares out the window. The swimming pool isn't visible from here, even if it weren't nighttime and the landscape weren't covered in dust. I know what she's seeing: the pool, that pool, again. Sunny floating face down, dead, or maybe not yet.

Jamie turns and looks directly at me. "I chose my future over hers, Beth. And there's not a day that's gone by since that I haven't known I made the wrong choice."

39

ROXY

Well, if this doesn't change everything. I didn't kill Sunny, Jamie did. Hallelujah. I mean, sure, it's still sad and horrible, and sure, she most likely ended up in the pool thanks to the margarita à la Roxy, but I wasn't the one who stood there and watched as she drowned. Relief washes over me, and as it does, I feel something else: a glimmer of myself returning. And that feels fabulous. I need to find Ryan and tell him the news.

It wasn't me. I didn't kill Sunny after all.

"Well, this has been such an evening, and we haven't even had dinner yet," I say. "Shall I ring the bell and ask for the rest of the meal to be served?"

"You can't seriously be hungry right now," Beth says, staring at me accusingly. A tear spills from her eye and works its way down her cheek.

"Maybe not, but Amelia must be famished. You look

anorexic, by the way," I tell her. And she does. It's been bothering me this entire weekend. I'm supposed to be the thinnest and the richest. Anyway, I digress.

"I'm not anorexic," Amelia slurs as she manages to return to her seat. "Nice try, though. You're still in the hot seat, Roxy, even if Jamie killed her."

"Well, we'll agree to disagree, as always. But the fact is you also should be relieved, Amelia. You might have lost your cash cow in me, but now you've got a new golden goose to extort." I point to the only doctor in the house. Ironic that she killed someone.

"Why would Jamie pay me?" Amelia says. "Oh, because she didn't save Sunny, and she doesn't want anyone outside this room to know it. Gotcha."

"Fortunately, she makes a fine living as a cardiologist, so she should be able to step into those monthly payments, no problem," I say. Jamie lets out a small squeak but doesn't try to protest.

Beth stands, hands on hips. "How can you talk like this, talk about Sunny like this? I never really knew any of you, did I? None of you are what you seem."

Amelia smiles at Beth and holds up her wineglass. "Haven't you figured it out by now, Beth? That's the Theta Gamma Mu way. None of us are what we seem. Could you pour me some wine, dear?"

I smile at both of them. "Well, somehow Beth here comes across as the saint in all this, smelling like a rose as always. She's always been exactly what she seemed," I say. "Boring to the bitter end, but at least she isn't a killer like Jamie."

Beth's face is blanched white, and she looks like she's going to faint. She begins to speak, opens her mouth, but nothing comes out. Clearly, she's still processing the fresh shock of Jamie's confession.

"Oh, fine," Amelia says, standing. "I'll get my own bloody refill."

The only sound in the room is the gurgling of the wine pouring into the glass. Amelia walks back to the table, studying Jamie as she sits in her chair, head down.

"Here's what I don't understand, Jay," Amelia says. "Were you so uptight around Brett this weekend because you thought he'd recognize you from our college days? I mean, that was a long time ago. But I guess you had to be worried he could, if he recognized you, expose your past drug use. I guess that could be a problem for a doctor."

Jamie looks up at Amelia. I watch her face fall again.

"What is it?" I ask her. "What's wrong now?"

Jamie tilts her head back, stares up at the ceiling, and then returns her gaze to Amelia. "I wasn't worried about him recognizing me from back in college. I knew he would recognize me. Because he's still my dealer. Or was."

40

AMELIA

I can't help but gasp as the pieces fall into place. It all makes perfect sense. No wonder Brett made such a point of flirting with Jamie as soon as he arrived. And during the pickleball tournament, even forcing her to be his partner. He'd been toying with her, enjoying the fact that he had a connection to her that no one else knew about, that no one else could know about. What a jerk. And I'm the idiot who brought him along this weekend. I wonder if that's the entire reason he came with me—to torment Jamie.

Jamie sits in her chair, still as a statue, staring at the table in front of her. Part of me wants to go to her side and give her a hug. But that's a very small part of me, so I stay put. Plus, with all this wine in my system, that's a long way down the table to travel. I cannot believe Brett. And here I thought he was just a pretty face to have fun with over the weekend.

"You're an addict?" Roxy says with a bit too much joy in her voice.

Across the table from me, Beth bites her lip, lost in thought.

"I'm an addict," Jamie says. "I tried to quit after Sunny died, but I couldn't. I graduated addicted. I went through med school addicted, started my career addicted. And I still am, to this day. Last month, I decided to try to get clean and wean myself off the drugs, but Brett didn't like that idea, not at all."

"So he came here to give you a message, didn't he?" I ask. And here I thought he was actually into me. I'm an idiot.

"Yep, I'm one of his biggest customers," Jamie says. "He told me he was here to send me a message, to let me know he'd ruin my life and expose my addiction if I didn't keep buying pills from him."

"What a piece of shit," I say. "I really had no idea about all of this."

"I know you didn't," Jamie says. "I'm good at hiding this part of my life, from everyone."

"But how do you hold it all together? Your job, your kids? And Greer doesn't know?" Beth says. "I don't understand."

"I've gotten skilled at hiding, like most addicts. We're sneaky," she says. "I never stopped, couldn't stop. And Brett was there all along. As a pharmacist, he has easy access to what I need. We even work for the same hospital system."

I try to see the addict in Jamie, but all I see is her outward perfection, her career, her loving family. "I don't know how you're doing this," I say. "I mean, everybody knows I have too much of this stuff." I hold up my glass of wine. "I wouldn't be able to hide this from anyone."

"Well, I have had a lot of practice managing to show up for my patients, my kids, my husband. I convinced myself I could keep my two lives separate," she says. She looks up from the table, tears in her eyes. "I even had sex with Brett sometimes, when I was short on cash. It was part of the price I had to pay to keep my life running smoothly."

Whoa. I mean, we did have fun fooling around, but I didn't need to have sex with Brett for drugs. That's a whole other level. And I don't want to think about them together.

"Brett kept making remarks to you. I heard him," I say. "It was irritating me, but it must have terrified you. All those little digs about how you're such a rule follower, what a great doctor you are, how lucky Greer is."

"He was warning me. Letting me know he had the power to expose me to Greer, to all of you, for the fraud that I am," Jamie says with a sad shrug.

"What a jerk," I say. "Sounds like he deserved to die."

"Amelia! Stop that," Beth says as a loud snap echoes overhead.

A deafening crack reverberates through the night. We all freeze in disbelief as a cacophony of destruction tears through the air. The ceiling groans and gives way under the weight of a falling giant tree, and shards of plaster rain down like confetti as the tree crashes through, its branches shattering the tablescape. Crystal glasses clatter against fine china, and the floral arrangements are reduced to chaos in an instant. The tree brings with it a cascade of debris and leaves, creating a whirlwind of broken branches entwined with shattered glass.

I hear myself screaming as the lights go out and the dining room is plunged into darkness. I crawl out from under the tree, scrambling to safety before there's another loud crack and the tree trunk falls through the roof and onto the dining room table. I hope everyone else managed to get out of there unscathed. I don't really know, though. I was too busy saving myself. Self-preservation is a vital life skill, one I've been utilizing this entire, chaotic weekend.

41

BETH

I know I'm in shock because everything happening is taking place in slow motion. I hold my hands up to my face. Maybe this is a nightmare? I fold my hands together. It's real. I've never been so terrified in my life. A huge tree narrowly missed crushing us all, and now we need to get out of here. The dining room, once a sparkling haven, is now a blend of destruction and the raw power of the fallen tree that has reshaped it.

Roxy sits in her chair at the end of the table, and Jamie sits next to her. Across the table from me, Amelia stands blinking.

"Roxy! Jamie! Amelia! We have to go, now!" I yell.

Amelia runs out of the room, but Jamie remains frozen in her seat. I run to Roxy, and she points to her arm.

"I'm stuck," she says, eyes wide with fear.

I see part of the tree, a large branch, has pinned Roxy's arm to the table. Somehow, I find superhuman strength and lift the tree branch.

"Move, Roxy, now," I say, holding the branch.

She pulls her arm out from under the branch as my strength gives out. I notice a large gash on her arm as I grab her by the shoulder. "We need to get out of here."

Roxy nods and stands up, finally ready to go.

"Jamie, come on," I say, taking her roughly by the arm. I hurry from the room as the ceiling groans again under the weight of the tree. As we make it to the foyer, I hear another deafening crack, and I know the entire trunk has crashed through the ceiling. I can't believe how close we all came to dying, right there, in the opulent dining room now in ruins.

By the time I usher Jamie and Roxy into the living room, Amelia greets me, her navy dress torn and disheveled, her expression a mix of shock and disbelief. She is staring at the piano where Brett's body lies covered by a sheet, like a sleeping ghost. What a catastrophe.

"Jamie, Roxy needs medical care," I say, hoping to snap her back to life, back to her career.

Jamie nods. "Yes, of course. Roxy, let me see that arm. Please."

"OK, but I think I need to lie down," Roxy says, dropping to the floor. Roxy's dress is covered in blood now, and Jamie makes quick work of ripping the bottom of her dress to make a bandage. Outside the wind has stopped, but that clearly doesn't mean we're out of danger. I hope another tree doesn't decide to smash into us, its roots, firmly entrenched in the earth for decades, breaking free tonight.

Jamie tends to Roxy's arm as Ryan and Greer rush into the room.

"Is everyone all right?" Ryan asks, hurrying to Roxy and Jamie. "Roxy, what happened?"

"A tree fell through the ceiling," she says. "My arm was pinned."

"She's going to be fine, but it will need medical treatment," Jamie says.

Greer walks to Jamie's side. I watch as they have an awkward embrace. "I'm glad you're all right. When we heard that loud crash, well, I thought the worst. We'll get through this, Jamie."

And as I watch their love story hold firm, I get angry. Greer doesn't know the worst of it, though, because he left the dining room before her full confession. He doesn't know that Jamie left Sunny to die in the pool. That she could have saved her.

"I love you," Jamie says, and they kiss.

I turn away, disgusted, I guess, with who Jamie really is, and was.

"Honey, could you go to our room, get my medical bag so I can treat and wrap Roxy's arm? She's going to need stitches," Jamie turns back to the patient, patting Roxy's shoulder.

"Yes, now that you two lovebirds have reunited, I'd love to stop bleeding out," Roxy says, the drama queen returning.

"Be right back with it," Greer says and disappears into the dark house using his phone's flashlight to show the way. I wouldn't want to go back down those hallways. The hole in the roof has allowed dust and debris to circulate through the house, I'm sure, reaching us here in this room now. My chest is tight with dust inhalation.

"OK, all right, everyone is alive, thank God," Ryan says, visibly stunned. His hair is a mess and his tie is missing. He wraps an arm around my shoulders. "Beth, are you sure you're OK?"

I'm likely in shock. "Fine, yes, it could have been much worse. Where are the kids?" I ask.

"We need to find them," Ryan says. "I'm worried the house isn't structurally stable given what's happened. We need to keep everyone in this original part of the house—here in the living room is best—until the roads are cleared and power is restored and we can call for help. I never should have allowed Roxy to invite all of you here. This weekend has ruined everything. I tried to warn you."

"What? Warn me? I haven't spoken to you for decades. What are you talking about?" I ask, but Ryan takes off down the hallway without answering. I follow behind him, holding on to the back of his coat for comfort and closeness. As we walk through the darkness, the air thick with dust, I wonder what Celeste and Zach have overheard tonight. Were they listening to our dining room conversation? I wonder what Ryan has heard, what he thinks, what he knows. There'll be time for that, I suppose, but first we need to find my daughter.

As we pass by the dining room my eyes try to make out the shape of the table, but all I can see is the large silhouette of the tree. And something else through the haze of dust and tree limbs. It's a face, a woman's face, staring at me from on top of the table. She is lying on top of the tree, on top of the table. Oh my God.

"Ryan!" I yell. "Someone is there. In the dining room!" I yank on his jacket, and he finally stops. He shines the light of his phone into the room, and a surreal sight appears amid the swirling dust. I catch a glimpse of a woman with long blond hair, green eyes, wearing a green dress and a sparkling tennis necklace.

42

BETH

"Oh my God," I say, backing up, backing away from the horror in the dining room.

"What is it?" he asks, turning the light to shine into my eyes.

"It's dressed like her, like Sunny, the night she died," I babble, my head spinning as I step away, holding my hand up to block the light from his phone.

"Relax, Beth. You're seeing things. Stress will do that to some people, drive them crazy," Ryan says. "We need to find the kids."

I turn back to look at the dining room, to find the woman, to find Sunny, but without Ryan's phone flashlight, it's too dark to see her. Something is very wrong. With everyone in this house. I need to find my daughter, and we need to get out of here.

"Celeste!" I yell, coughing and choking on dust as we make our way to the kitchen. "Celeste! Where are you?"

"Mom!" Celeste yells. "We're in here. Inside the pantry." We watch a door open, and she and Zach are revealed, wide-eyed but fine. Celeste gives me a big hug and takes my hand. "I was so scared."

"So was I, but we're going to be fine. We need to stay together," I say. *And we need to get out of here as soon as we can*, I don't say.

"OK, let's get you back to the other part of the house," Ryan says, wrapping Zach in a hug and leading the way. "I'm not sure this addition, this part of the house is safe. It may have been compromised when the tree fell through the roof."

"Wow, that's what happened? The noise was crazy. See, I told you we'd be fine," Zach says to Celeste. "Your mom and my dad to the rescue."

"Let's take them to my room; it's part of the original house, right?" I ask Ryan. I'd like to avoid going the same way we came because I don't want to see *her* again. A chill runs down my spine, but I stay strong. For Celeste. I also don't want to go back to the living room with all my so-called sisters and the dead body adorning the piano. I want to get to our room, find my car keys, and hit the road—travel warning be damned.

"Sure, yes, that works. Let's go to your room," he says, and we walk quickly in a tight group to get there. When we finally reach the door and hurry inside, it's a surreal world of calm on the other side of the hallway.

I turn on my phone flashlight and shine it at Celeste, making sure she's unharmed. Her pink dress is now coated in dust and dirt like everyone else's. I have twigs and leaves in my hair, scratches on my arm. But we're safe.

"Well, looks like this engagement party is over," I say as a wave of relief fills my heart. "Maybe I'll host one for you. Back home. Nothing fancy, full of friends and love. We can take our time. No rush." I'm still not sure what's going on here, with Ryan and Gentry House, but it's creeping me out. Did I really see Sunny darting through the dining room? No, it was my mind playing tricks on me, it must have been.

"Sounds good to me," Zach says. "This weekend was all my mom's idea, as you all know."

"A bad one," Ryan says with a frown. "As usual."

I look at Ryan, his face uplit by his phone's flashlight, distorted by the light, half illuminated in the darkness, and for once, I see him as a stranger. I don't want to stay in this room with him. I don't want Celeste in here, but it's safer here than near the collapsing roof. And Zach is here with her. He loves her, or does he? I'm having my doubts about him, and about this entire family.

I walk to the bathroom and splash water on my face, cleaning the grit and grime from my eyes, nose, and mouth as much as I can. I dry my face with a washcloth. And that's when I see the letter, taped to my mirror. It's typed.

Dear Beth,

Oh, how I've missed you all these years. You were my best friend, the one person I could trust no matter what.

But now, everything has changed. This is all your fault. You never should have come here. To my home. You weren't there for me the night I died, were you? No, you weren't. I know where you were. And now you come to my home and ruin everything good and pure. Do you feel guilty, Beth? Do you? You should. You took everything from me, but you won't do it again. Go away, Beth.

My hands shake as the note drops to the bathroom counter. My stomach clenches when I see the scrawled signature at the bottom of the letter. My heart races.

Love, Sunny

No. This is not from my dead best friend. It can't be. Sunny's ghost is haunting me? Me? I look at myself in the mirror. "I'm sorry, Sunny," I say to my reflection. *I loved you, I still love you.* I pick up the note again.

Do I feel guilty?

I bang my hands on the bathroom counter. This isn't Sunny's note. It's from somebody alive and not well. I take a deep breath and walk back into the room.

"You know what, I'm going to go check on the others. Jamie may need my help with Roxy because Amelia is no help, as usual," I say, grabbing my purse. I'm going to try to find out if the driveway is passable, if my car is OK or damaged by the storm. "Ryan, could you stay here, with these two?"

"Of course I could, but I think maybe I should go with you," he says and walks me to the door. He puts his hand on my shoulder. It should be a comforting gesture, but it's not, not anymore. But I smile. I need to keep him happy, on my side, until we leave.

"I'll be right back," I say and pat his hand.

"Be careful out there. And do not go near the dining room. If you need me, I'll be right here waiting for you. With Celeste."

I know he added her name as a warning. I know. Message received, loud and clear. I have one more question I need answered, and unfortunately, the answer is in the living room with one of my sisters.

43

BETH

I find Jamie, Roxy, and Amelia exactly where I left them. Jamie
has bandaged Roxy's arm, and Amelia has found some sort of
alcohol that was stashed in a fancy decanter and is busy regaling
Roxy with some story or another, while trying to give her a drink.

"It will help with the pain," Amelia says. Her red hair is wild
around her shoulders from the wind, and she looks like a tempt-
ress in her slinky navy dress. Her wiles are not working on Roxy,
though.

I glance across the room at the body on the piano, thankful
I covered him with a sheet. I'm standing next to Jamie, who is
kneeling on the ground cleaning up her medical supplies, tucking the unused things away.

"Do you always travel with that?" I ask.

"I do. You never know when an emergency might happen,"
she says.

"Where's Greer?" I ask. He's the only one who is missing.

"He went to get help. He said he's tired of being stuck here. He feels trapped, and, well, I don't think he wants to be around me right now. Maybe not ever again," Jamie says. "I told him it was too dangerous outside, that trees are down, power lines, too, and who knows if the fire is contained yet. He said he felt safer going to get help than being here."

"Yes, well, it has been a night of revelations," I say. And then I drop my voice. The real reason I had to find Jamie and confront her, one last time. "You know, I was thinking it was convenient for Brett to die before he could expose you and your drug use to the group."

Jamie flinches and closes her medical bag. She doesn't look up at me.

"Unless it wasn't an accident. Is there something else you want to tell us?" I ask. This gets Roxy's and Amelia's attention, and they are by my side, circling Jamie, like they smell blood in the water.

Jamie shakes her head. "Haven't there been enough confessions tonight?"

"My God, Jamie, tell us what you did," Roxy says, waving her bandaged arm around. "What have you got to lose? I mean, Greer seems to still love you, despite what you are. Meanwhile, Ryan hates me. And, well, Amelia here, she's basically unlovable. And Beth's not exactly the poster child for happily-ever-after either."

"Shut up, Roxy," Amelia says.

I focus on Jamie, my phone light pointed at her face like a searchlight. I'm searching for the truth, and then Celeste and I are getting out of here. "Tell us."

For a moment I think she's going to refuse again, but then her body sags and she lets out a long sigh. We have her surrounded. She has no choice.

"He was going to ruin my life. He as much as said so when we were alone, before the pickleball games. He said we better sleep together this weekend, or he would spill the beans," Jamie said. "He was horrible, and he deserved to die. I injected his Gatorade with potassium chloride; I carry it around in my medical bag. It's an essential tool to save lives."

"Um, it had the opposite effect, it seems," Amelia says, stumbling a little as she tries to stand still. She takes a big sip of whatever it is she's having now. "He was a rather rotten bastard, wasn't he?"

"Yes, he was. I know I'm responsible for my own addiction, but he preyed on my vulnerabilities and constantly found ways to push pills on me. He worked hard to keep me addicted all these years."

She pauses, looking at each of us, I guess hoping we'll see her, not the addict, the sorority sister. I do see her.

"I hope you know we're here for you—we are," I say.

Jamie smiles at me. "I hope you will be."

"You've now let Sunny die and killed Brett. How exactly should we be there for you?" Roxy says, an edge to her voice. She does have a point.

"Oh, come on, tell us already," Amelia says, clearly enjoying herself. "When did you decide to off him?"

"I decided to do it at breakfast. I decided to kill Brett," Jamie says, remembering and wincing.

"Wow, bold," Amelia says. "How'd you do it?"

Jamie wraps her arms around herself, reluctant to tell us the truth. But finally, she begins to talk.

"After breakfast I went back to our room and grabbed my syringe. In predictable Brett fashion he brought his own supersized water bottle, custom-engraved with his initials, to the pickleball court. I watched as he dumped two bottles of Gatorade into it and twisted the lid."

"He did have too many things with his initials on them. It was weird," Amelia says.

I give her the stink eye. She needs to be quiet. "Jamie, go on."

"It was hot out, and I knew he'd chug down his bottle while we played. He even had the gall to threaten me during the game, telling me if we didn't win, my secrets were out," Jamie says.

"So when he crossed to the other side of the court to help Ryan fix the net height, I pushed the syringe of potassium chloride into his monogrammed bottle." She stands up and faces the three of us. "I killed him. That's the truth. I chose to protect my own future, just like I did with Sunny." She glances at the body under the sheet across the room and then turns back to us.

A chill has shot through the air between us. I can't believe what she did. I don't understand. "How does potassium chloride kill people?" I ask. I wonder again how I could be sisters with a murderer, a repeat murderer like Jamie. First Sunny, now Brett. And she's supposed to save lives. Is it any wonder I've kept my distance from this crowd for twenty-five years?

"Brett's shortness of breath at the end of lunch was the first symptom caused by the drug. When he rushed outside, I knew he didn't have long to live," Jamie says. "The fresh air he was looking for wasn't going to prevent his impending heart attack, which happened and caused him to fall into the pool. He was dead when he hit the water."

"God, Jamie, are you listening to yourself?" I say. She's so calm and composed you'd think she was talking about buying groceries, not ending a life.

"So, you pretended to try to save him by jumping into the pool and then doing CPR, under the cover of all that dust," Amelia says, putting her hand on Roxy's shoulder to stop wobbling.

"I was making sure he died, yes," Jamie says. "I performed CPR to be certain I pushed the drug all the way in his system. I knew I'd given him a fatal dose. The CPR helped it work faster. Oh, and I'm not sorry."

"I can tell," I say.

"There is no way to prove it, though," Jamie says. "It's out of his bloodstream by now. Cause of death will be a stopped heart due to cardiac arrest."

"Oh my God," Roxy says. "Who are we? We can turn you in; we can tell the authorities everything you've done. It could be enough."

"Please, you have to believe me—it was the only way. He came here to threaten me, and he did," Jamie says. "He was never going to let me go. I didn't have a choice. It was the only way."

"What a convenient way to murder someone, Jamie. I'm impressed. And I am sorry I brought him, the bastard," Amelia says. "I should have left well enough alone. Still, you shouldn't resort to murder."

"It was the only way to get free," Jamie says, tears rolling down her cheeks. "You have to believe me. He was a monster. Please, don't turn me in."

"I can't believe this," I say. I stare at Jamie as if she were a stranger. She is a stranger.

"Brett was a jerk. He probably did deserve it. And, Amelia, you weren't even supposed to be here, let alone bring a plus-one," Roxy says. "You brought him to upset me, test me. You knew I'd remember buying the roofies from him, and you wanted to throw me off my game. It's really your fault he's dead."

"Well, that's a stretch. Sorry, I am not going to be the one guilty of murder. That's the Rock Star doctor's charge," Amelia says. "Roxy, the truth is, really, I wasn't thinking about you. It was all about me. I thought he was into me. I wanted to flaunt a red-hot romance in front of you guys. But now I know he was using me to get to Jamie. To give her a warning. I'm an idiot."

I turn to look at Jamie and then at the other two. They really are unbelievable. Instead of truly sticking together all these years, honoring the memory of Sunny and our sorority bonds, they've been competing, cheating, and ultimately, killing.

44

BETH

This all ends here and now. We need to come together, or we'll all be ruined.

"It's time to reach an understanding, among the four of us, right now, right here," I say. "Jamie, you need help, treatment, not jail time. So here's the deal I'm putting on the table. We all will keep this our secret—*without* profiting from it, Amelia—as long as you agree to get help for your addiction."

Silence falls over the room, and then one by one, Roxy, Amelia, and finally Jamie nod in agreement. I should make them sign something, I suppose, or do a finger-prick blood oath, but there isn't time.

"Beth, you are giving me more mercy than I deserve," Jamie says. "Thank you."

Roxy smiles at me. "I'm impressed, Beth. Maybe there's more Theta Gamma Mu in you than I thought."

I shake my head and smile. "God, I hope not." I'm only partially kidding.

And now, my final question of the night. "Have any of you felt at all threatened since you arrived at Gentry House? Anything weird happen? Any unexplainable situations?"

Roxy looks at me and tilts her head. "You mean other than my marriage imploding, my houseguest dying, my roof caving in, and my deepest darkest secrets exposed to people I'm not sure I can trust? I'd say that's enough weirdness for one weekend, thank you very much." Something on my face must tell her I'm not kidding, because her expression sobers. "Why do you ask, Beth? What's happened?"

"I found a letter, just now, typed but signed with Sunny's signature. Sunny's handwriting! I recognize it now, all these years later. It was taped to my bathroom mirror. She told me she missed me but that I should let go now and leave this place," I say, swallowing the fear rising in my throat.

"What? Why didn't you say something sooner?" Roxy asks. "Can you show me the letter?"

"It's in my room. But Ryan is in there, too, with the kids, so I left it there," I say. "It was the same writing as the postcard in my bedside table. It disappeared the same day it arrived," I say.

Amelia says, "What postcard? You never mentioned that."

"I know, I should have. I opened the drawer of the bedside table and found a postcard. The photo on it was of a woman, shot from behind, dangling her legs in the pool. She had long blond hair. She wore a green bathing suit," I say.

"Oh my God," Roxy says. "How creepy."

"This isn't right," Jamie says.

"And then there was the newspaper hidden beneath a coffee table book," I say, a chill rolling down my spine. "The newspaper story, the one from the *Palm Springs Register* about Sunny's death."

"What? Why didn't you say something?" Amelia asks. "Do you still have it?"

"No, it's gone, disappeared," I say. "I mean, I figured maybe Ryan had kept it as a memento or something, but then it vanished."

"I want to get out of here," Jamie says. "Roxy, you need to leave too. We all do."

"I don't know what to do," Roxy says, smoothing her hair, removing a twig.

"Roxy, have you been receiving any of these notes or cards or anything?" I ask.

Roxy takes a deep breath. "Everything is strange. It's like this whole house is a monument to her, to Sunny," she says, cradling her bandaged arm. Her lavender dress is streaked with dirt and her own blood. She looks like an actor in a horror movie. Maybe she is.

"This is creepy," Jamie says, her eyes darting to Brett's body and back to us. "All of it."

"I know. You're right. I felt it from the minute we pulled in the driveway," I say. "And Roxy, I'm afraid Ryan bought this place for Sunny. To remember Sunny. To enshrine her in the last place she was alive. He won't admit it, though, not even to himself, if I had to guess."

Roxy nods. "He did it on purpose. He knows what he's done. It's been his obsession since he bought the place. She's been his obsession since she died. I tried to ignore it, to deny the truth. But I can't any longer."

"Oh God, a husband obsessed with a dead college girlfriend. That's a lot," Amelia says.

"The worst of it, though," Roxy says, "is I've seen her here. She's here."

45

ROXY

The three women stare at me now, clearly waiting for me to explain. But I can't. It doesn't make any sense, but yet, she's here. She has been since we arrived, and I suppose she will be here long after we leave this place. I cannot wait to get out of here. Ryan can have Gentry House, and all the ghosts he's conjured to fill it. He's right. It is time for a divorce. I'll be a lonely woman who's staring down the wrong side of fifty, but at least I'm not living with a ghost.

"To be clear, until this weekend, I would tell you I don't believe in ghosts," I say. "But I've seen Sunny, several times now. The first time was right after we arrived, before you got here. She was on the driveway, some distance from me, and walking in the opposite direction. She had the same long blond hair, the same green dress she always loved wearing."

"What? It can't be Sunny," Amelia says. "We all know

what happened to her. Read the paper, for heaven's sake. I need another drink."

"I know Sunny's dead," I tell her. "I caused it."

"We both did," Jamie says. "Where else did you see her?"

"There was a photo in my bedside table," I say, my voice shaking. "It was of a young woman, wearing a tiny bikini like Sunny's, sitting by the pool, kicking her feet in the water. It was black and white, but still you could tell it was her."

"From spring break?" I ask. "That was like the postcard in my room. I thought it was her."

"No, it was this pool. The Gentry House pool, so it couldn't be from spring break," Roxy says, her eyes huge. "I screamed when I saw the photo and slammed the dresser drawer. I ran to find Ryan, to ask him if he placed it there. He looked at me like I was crazy. Really, the way he has looked at me for the last few years. With contempt. When I finally convinced him to come see the photo later that evening, I opened the drawer, and it was gone."

The four of us are silent, wondering what all of this could mean, what we should do.

"We need to get out of here," Beth says. "I don't know what's going on, but we should all leave, as soon as we can. Ryan's playing tricks on us, for some reason. He might have a hologram projector, or who knows what else? Let's get going and figure things out later, from the safety of anywhere but here."

I agree. "But what about the engagement weekend?" I ask, but this time I smile. And start to laugh. At myself. At everything

I've been holding on to for too long. At the illusion of a perfect marriage, the illusion that this house was for us, when it was all for Ryan. And Sunny.

"What's so funny?" Amelia asks. "This is all spooky, if you ask me. I don't want Sunny's ghost haunting me."

"Well, since you didn't do anything to her, you're fine," Beth says and then eyes me and Jamie. "Jamie, any strange notes or ghost sightings? Or were you too busy planning Brett's demise to notice?"

"Funny," Jamie says, shaking her head. "There was one thing. A towel on our outside lounge chair."

"Let me guess," Beth says. "Pink-and-white-striped like they were at Desert Sunrise. And all the towels here at Gentry House are white, with blue trim."

Jamie nods. "I didn't say anything because, well, how do you explain something like that?"

"You can't," Beth says.

"But there has to be an explanation. Ghosts aren't real," Amelia says. "Someone is messing with us."

"Yes, someone has been messing with us," Beth says.

"He never wanted us to come here, to his place. I realize that now," I say, meeting Beth's eyes. "We should leave, as soon as it's safe, and never come back. I'm sorry I dragged you all here."

I'm sorry for all of it.

46

BETH

I want to tell them about the life-size mannequin dressed up like Sunny lying on top of the dining room table, but I'm not sure it was real. Maybe my mind was playing tricks on me. I decide to keep that rather creepy image to myself. I think we all know now what is going on.

"I need to go find Celeste, and we're leaving as soon as we can. All secrets stay between us, right? It's time to leave Ryan to his delusions," I say, looking them each in the eye. "And let's not get together again anytime soon."

"Good idea," Amelia says. "Bad things happen when we're all together. We need to forget all about what's happened here. I know I plan to. Maybe I already have."

"You're in no shape to drive, Amelia," Jamie says. "Greer and I will give you a ride home, as long as you keep your mouth shut."

"I'm not sure that's possible," Amelia says with a deep chuckle. "I'm fine to drive; I really am."

"I'm alone as of this weekend, if you change your mind," Roxy says, her voice tinged with pain. "I can't believe my marriage imploded like this, in front of you all. But I'll be fine, I think. I hope."

"You're stronger than you think you are," Jamie says. "I hope to prove I am too."

Roxy smiles. "You will. As for Ryan, I think it's for the best."

"Definitely for the best," I say. "OK, let's get going."

I find Celeste and Zach in my room where I left them, but Ryan is gone.

"Where's Ryan?" I ask, keeping my voice calm as I begin to pack. "Celeste, we can send for your things. Yours, too, Zach. We're leaving now."

"Mom, we can take a few minutes to pack. I need my stuff," Celeste says. "Zach and I will start packing. You should too."

"OK, but don't go near the dining room," I say. "And we are leaving as soon as it's safe." The storm is over, but the air is still tense with the raging fires. The aftermath of today will take years to clean up. Some lives will be changed forever, I know that. But it's hard to think about the future when I have a more pressing concern: One of my sorority sisters is a murderer, the other drugged my best friend, and a third extorted the second. And then there's this creepy place and its resident ghost.

I hear a quiet knock on the door. I've been expecting it, I guess. I've changed into my typical at-home uniform of sweatpants and a sweatshirt. I did my best to wipe the grime from my face, but I'll wait until I'm back home to shower. I've tossed everything into my suitcase, and I'm ready to go. I wheel the suitcase to the door and open it.

"Leaving a day early?" Ryan says. "I can't say I blame you. But the roads aren't cleared yet, so you might as well relax, and stay awhile."

"What do you want, Ryan?" I say, stepping aside as he walks in, crosses the room to the fireplace, and takes a seat in one of the comfy white chairs facing the fire. I've put the note from Sunny on the dresser, and he eyes it but doesn't say anything.

"It's nice the gas lines are still working," he says. "Otherwise, we'd all be suffering through a cold night. There's been enough suffering this weekend, wouldn't you agree?"

"I would. Why did you let Roxy invite us here, to your special house?" I ask, refusing to sit in the chair facing his. I'm ready to bolt out of the room if anything strange or ghostly happens.

"Greer didn't make it far in his quest for help, so he's back, and he and Jamie went to their room," he says, ignoring my question. "I guess they still have a chance of staying together. But she needs help. Anyway, you're not going anywhere, not anytime soon."

She's not the only one, I think, studying Ryan.

"Yes, Jamie agreed to go to a treatment program, so I hope she'll be OK," I say. I am glad Ryan doesn't know any more about Jamie than what happened with Sunny. He doesn't need to know she killed Brett. The Sunny situation, that's enough.

I cross my arms and stare at Ryan. Flames from the fireplace send shadows dancing through the room. Memories of that night begin to flash through my head again, more unwelcome ghosts of the past, of *that* past. That night. I've been so careful not to dwell on it over the last twenty-five years. But being here, in this house, with these people, it's like all my protective walls have come crumbling down. Ryan's face morphs into his younger self, the person I remember, far different from the man he has become. But back then, the last night of spring break, he was more than cute Ryan, my best friend's boyfriend.

The stars were out, and we'd all finished dining alfresco. All of us except Sunny.

Amelia wore a dress from Roxy's closet, which surprised me at the time since Roxy was a notorious non-sharer of clothes. Probably because she had the best.

"Come on, you have to go out. It's our last night," Amelia coaxed, plopping her napkin on her plate and pushing it to the middle of the table. We'd all been drinking margaritas as we ate our dinner, and we were all well on our way to drunk.

"I'll go if you go," Jamie said, leaning her head on my shoulder, already tipsy.

"Sure, I guess," I'd said, and I'd looked over at Ryan for some reason, and he smiled.

"I'll come along too," he said. "You all need an escort, for sure."

"Are you sure you don't want to stay here, Ryan, enjoy our

last night at the Desert Sunrise?" Roxy asked. "I mean, the pool is so warm. Let's go swimming?"

Ryan tilted his head. "I think the casino is a great call. We should all go."

"Sure, great, a casino." Roxy seemed to be beyond excited by that announcement. "I'm coming, too, then."

I shake my head at the memory. The last night was a disaster, for the most part. As soon as we arrived at the casino, Amelia disappeared to go find the guys she was flirting with, Roxy slipped away doing who knows what, and Jamie excused herself, telling me she had something to do. And Ryan, he'd headed to the blackjack table, he said, to try to win some bucks.

I couldn't believe I was alone, in a casino. I didn't have money to waste on gambling, and now, I didn't have a single friend by my side. I missed Sunny, and I decided to grab a cab and head back to the hotel. I made my way to the outdoor bar and ordered the usual, a margarita. I decided I'd have one more drink to end my spring break before reality set in the next day.

"Come here often, beautiful?" a man said, touching my shoulder in a too-familiar gesture. My neck tensed and my fists clenched.

I turned, ready to punch him, when I realized it was Ryan. "Hi," I said through my drunken haze.

"Hey," he said. "I lost all my money over there at the blackjack table, but on the plus side they do give you free drinks."

"Good to know," I answered. The fact that I was also out of money, the money Sunny had borrowed for me from the sorority, was weighing heavily on me by that time of the night. I was so lucky she had brought me on the trip. I had to make it back to school without needing to ask for more. The bartender walked by, and Ryan signaled for two more margaritas.

"I'm not going to be able to walk to my room if I drink another one," I said.

Ryan draped his arm over my shoulders and leaned in close. "Don't worry. I'll escort you to your room. You're safe with me."

47

BETH

My heart banged in my chest. Was he flirting with me? No, of course not. He loved Sunny. I loved Sunny. We were close friends, like you are when you like your best friend's boyfriend. Nothing more.

"You're really very pretty, Beth," Ryan had said. "You don't make a point of standing out, though. You hide yourself, hide your beauty. Most of the sorority members, they show off. You aren't like them."

I know I smiled and showed my dimple before self-consciously turning away. I'd never had this kind of attention from a man like Ryan.

The bartender placed our next round of margaritas in front of us. My head felt dizzy; my heart felt a buzzy happiness. But this was wrong, I told myself: He was Sunny's boyfriend.

"Sunny is very pretty, and Sunny never shows off," I said. I took a sip of my unneeded drink. The salt stung my sunburned lip, but I was beyond feeling pain.

"Sunny is just that. But so are you," Ryan said. He stood then and searched his pockets.

"What are you doing?" I asked as I watched him recheck his pockets.

"Well, it's odd, but I can't find my room key," he said. "I swear I had it at dinner. It must have slipped out of my pocket. Shit. The office will be closed by the time we get back, and I don't want to wake Sunny by knocking on our door. Guess I'm bunking in the lobby tonight."

I smiled. He was a friend. I had my own room. "OK, listen, you can sleep in my room as long as you agree to stay on your side of the bed. And you better not snore."

Ryan raised his margarita, his blue eyes sparkling. "I promise. Thank you. You're a good friend."

But I wasn't. We woke up the next morning, groggy and hungover. We promised never to speak of it, and never to repeat it. But I never forgot it.

"That night…" Ryan says now, breaking into my memories. I look at him, so handsome then, so different now, sitting in the chair across from me, in my room, yet again.

"We both loved her. We need to focus on that," I say and take a deep breath. I don't want to talk about Sunny, not until I'm far away from here and her ghost. And I don't want to discuss that night.

"But if I hadn't slept in your room," he says and pushes his hand through his hair. I can see the pain in his eyes.

"Stop. Sunny's death was a tragedy, Ryan, but it wasn't your fault," I say. "Please, focus on the future, on Zach, and the wedding of our fabulous kids."

Ryan smiles, stands, and takes a step closer to me. "You know, I purchased this place as a penance for not being there for Sunny. I thought if I saved this place from being torn down, this place that looks too much like the Desert Sunrise, that if I saved it, I was saving her. I know it doesn't make any sense."

"None of it really makes sense," I say, taking a step back, away from him. "We all are doing the best we can."

"I plan to move here, full time, and try to remember the happy times, before she died, before everything changed," he says. "She's here, you know."

"No, you can't bring her back, as much as I'd like to. I think you need help," I say. "I miss her every day too. But, Ryan, you've taken this too far."

"No, she's here," he says. "You'll meet her someday soon. Maybe today."

Now he's lost it. I need to get out of here. People live their lives with all types of illusions and delusions. I guess whatever works, as long as it doesn't hurt anybody else. He's harmless, I remind myself as my heart thuds in my chest, a grieving, confused, and unhappy man.

Ryan starts talking again. "That's why I married Roxy, I guess. It was what I deserved for not being there for Sunny. I would suffer through a marriage of convenience with a woman

I could barely stand, to atone for my sins. Except Zach. He was an unforeseen blessing."

"Kids get you through a lot," I say. "It's been only me and Celeste, really from the beginning. I don't know what I would have done without her to care for. She gave my life purpose."

"You did a great job with her," Ryan says. "She's a remarkable young woman. Zach is a lucky guy."

"Thank you," I say and make a move toward the door. Celeste is getting married. I still cannot believe how fast life goes, how quickly she morphed from a colicky baby to a beautiful woman on the cusp of marriage.

"Beth," Ryan says, "you know it's over between Roxy and me. It has been, long before it even began. That's why this house, this remodel, and the love I found here have saved me."

"I was always surprised by that choice, when you decided to marry Roxy," I say. I thought, in my dreams perhaps, he would have picked me. Now I know I dodged a bullet.

"It was a bad choice, solely based on the pregnancy," he says. "I should have asked you on a date. You were Sunny's true friend, and mine too. I was so confused during that time, so sad."

He reaches his hand out to me. Every nerve ending in my body is screaming *run*. I take a deep breath. I don't want him to see my fear. I ignore his gesture but keep my eyes locked on his.

"But now here you are," he says. "Ironic, really, since you're the one who ruined everything. It was all your fault. If I hadn't been with you, Sunny would have lived."

I swallow. My fault. What to say? He is in love with a ghost, a vision of Sunny. I think about Sunny, her impish grin, the dazzling warmth of her presence, her sparkling green eyes and long blond hair. Her signature laugh that lit up the room. I look into his eyes, dark and simmering. He blames me for all of this? Incredible.

"Did you, um, make that mannequin, the one that fell from the sky?" I ask. I keep my tone calm, like this is a normal question.

48

BETH

When he finally decides to say something, his voice is odd, robotic.

"Sunny's memorial room is tucked away—well, it was— above the dining room, unfortunately," Ryan says. "There will be so much damage to sort through. Thank God she's OK, though. She wasn't in there when the tree fell. Look, Beth, I can't have you telling anyone about her. Not yet. I've got to get through the divorce. You understand."

"Sure, yes, your secret is safe with me," I say. Ryan moves in front of the door, blocking my exit. I walk across the room to the window. The morning sunrise sky is a bright yellow morphing into blue. What a welcome sight. It's time to go.

I turn around and bump into Ryan. He is standing too close. He grabs my shoulders.

"Do I scare you or something?" he says. "I thought you still had a crush on me, I really did. I thought you'd do anything for me, like you did that night all those years ago. I've been keeping tabs on you. Watching you, and Celeste. I wanted to reach out, but I was trapped by Roxy."

His fingers are digging into the top of my arms, and it hurts. I swallow, fear and panic zipping through me. Hopefully, Celeste and Zach will come check on me. "What do you want, Ryan?"

He releases one of my shoulders but steps forward and pins me against the window. He takes his phone out of his pocket. "I want you to meet Sunny."

49

AMELIA

Morning is my least favorite time of the day. I stretch and stifle a yawn, surprised I was able to sleep given the events of the night before. Sure, I acted freaked out like the rest of them, but I wasn't really.

As I hope you know by now, I am a great actress. I should have pursued that dream of moving to LA and auditioning until I made it. I would have made it. But my parents forbade it, and so I slumped into a traditional life as a wife and mother, eventually a DC socialite with no desires other than maintaining her appearance for as long as possible. But looks always fade, and nothing is as it appears.

I don't drink half as much as they think I do, at least not on a normal evening. But still, last night was a long one, and unnerving at that. Even I couldn't fake my way through it without some booze.

So, yes, I'm a bit hungover. OK, maybe a lot hungover. That's why I'm at the pool, on a lounge chair, waiting for one of Roxy's servers to bring me a Bloody Mary. A little hair of the dog, so to speak, before I head out.

The sun feels fabulous this morning, and despite the layer of dust and soot covering everything, I'm happy out here. I scraped the dirt and debris off the lounge chair with a broom I found in the pool house closet, grabbed a cute towel from my room, and voilà, perfection amid the chaos. That's me. Truth be told, I often cause the chaos that I'm surrounded by.

This whole weekend is a blur.

While I am lying on the lounge chair, I'm contemplating packing. If Brett were still alive, I would have begged him to throw all my stuff back in my suitcases. I hate that part of traveling. Back at home, my housekeeper packs for me and unpacks when I return. Yes, I'm spoiled, but I deserve it. I look down at my phone and open my photos. There's one of Brett and me, a selfie at breakfast yesterday morning. We still had the glow from sex. We looked good, and healthy. But now he's dead. I think about poor dead Brett, in repose on the piano. I wasn't sure what to do with his things, so I decided I would leave them as they are in the room we shared and get the heck out of there. After I pack, reluctantly, I'll summon one of Roxy and Ryan's servants to carry my Louis Vuitton bags to the car this time. I'll leave Brett and his baggage behind.

I'm also lying here reflecting on all the confessions of last night, amid the chaos of the storm and the tree falling through the dining room. These ladies sure do know how to spill the beans, and next thing you know, they all think they see Sunny everywhere they turn. That's silly. Ghosts haunt the ones who hurt them. That's their job.

Sunny should be haunting me, truth be told. I killed her. It was me. I got to her before Jamie ever saw her, and I made sure she died in that pool. Cold? Perhaps. But she was about to ruin my life.

You see, Sunny knew my big secret back then, senior year. I remember the moment she confronted me like it was yesterday. The tap on my shoulder that changed everything. I turned and there was Sunny. I put on my best blank face, but I knew what this would be about. I twirled one of my pigtails in my right hand, a nervous habit since childhood.

"Hey, I'm sorry to bring this up here, but I've had trouble finding you at the house," Sunny said. "You need to pay your dues, Amelia. You are two quarters behind, and we all know you have the money." Sunny's perfect hair spilled over her shoulders, and she wore a cute kelly-green sweater and jeans, not dressy, not fancy, but beautiful, naturally, as always. We'd all returned to campus after Christmas break. The chapter meeting was about to begin. I'd reluctantly attended because I didn't want a fine and because I am one of the queen bees of the sorority, so my absence would be noticed.

Girls were chatting about their breaks, how wonderful it had been to be home. Mine wasn't that wonderful; in fact, it was horrible. I'd arrived home from campus and walked into my family's regal Boston home. None of the lights were on, and my mother and father were sitting in their favorite chairs in the living room. Seemingly waiting for me, but they were in the dark. I started to turn on a light, but my father said, "Leave it. Sit down." So, I did, taking a chair across from them.

"There's no easy way to say this, Amelia, and I'm not sure of all the repercussions yet," my father said, "but we are ruined."

That was the moment my life fractured into before and after. The moment everything changed. "I don't understand, sir," I'd said.

"I've declared bankruptcy, Amelia. My family's textile industry has come to ruin in my hands," my father said as my mom sniffled quietly next to him. "I'll likely go to prison for a bit. But that's not your worry. I would suggest you graduate and get the hell away from us. Find a good man who can afford the lifestyle you're accustomed to."

I wanted to move to LA and be an actress. "Don't worry. I'll support myself in LA."

"Hogwash. You'll get married. Period. We have nothing to give you, not anymore. You will be destitute," he said. "You are not equipped to take care of yourself in LA or, well, anywhere. You need a rich man."

I'd never been anything but the rich girl. The rich girl with the best clothes, the fancy car, the biggest group of friends, the largest house. My mind wasn't processing what he said, so I simply nodded.

"You should go back to campus," my mother said. "It's

getting ugly here. Stay at the sorority house. Eat your meals there, as soon as they open back up from break. Theta Gamma Mus take care of each other. You'll be fine there."

And so I'd left and flew back to campus on Christmas Eve. No one else was at the house, but that was for the best. I couldn't face another person, not with what had happened, what I'd suddenly become. During those nights alone I decided no one must know. I would do my best acting job ever. And my performance impressed even me. My dad told me he'd take a plea deal and keep our family name out of the news. I hoped he was right. For my part, I would pretend as if nothing had changed.

I smiled in my best sorority recruitment grin as Sunny studied me carefully, the mask of friendship slipping onto my face. "Sure, I'm planning on it. Right after spring break, OK? My dad had to move some funds around," I said. "I don't really understand all the finances, but he said he'd take care of it."

Sunny had tilted her head, thinking, I suppose, about whether to believe me or not. Money was my superpower, and without it, I'd be nothing. None of these so-called sisters would like me once they knew I wasn't rich anymore. And the whole campus would find out soon enough. I could not allow that to happen. I had my blue-blooded pride to protect.

Bad news always spreads like wildfire. I refused to be the topic of the rumor mill. Gossip is only fun when it's not about you.

50

AMELIA

I stared at Sunny, looking straight into her green eyes. I had to make a calculation; I had to finagle a win for me, and I'd been thinking about it since I arrived back to campus on Christmas Eve. We were so close to graduation. I could max out my credit cards and fake it. It was only a few more months. No one would see me ruined. If I could get Sunny to keep her mouth shut for two more months, the Theta Gam budget would become the next treasurer's problem and we'd all be gone, graduated before my missing dues were even discovered. Win-win.

"Fine, but after spring break, I need it all paid in full. We have the spring formal to worry about. OK, great talk," Sunny said, breezing away from me with her all confident, Miss Popular casual style. Infuriating.

I needed more than the three months until after spring

break. I needed to fake it until we graduated in early June. "Sure, sounds great," I said to her back.

But still, I didn't plan on killing her. I'm not a monster. It just happened. An opportunity, and I was taught to seize opportunities. That night, the last night of spring break, I ditched Beth at the casino. You can't blame me; the place was full of hot guys, and I didn't want her around for competition. And it all worked out. I went home with a hottie who was staying at our same hotel. After he passed out, I decided to walk back to my own hotel room at the Desert Sunrise. Easier to avoid the awkward morning-after conversation that way. I was doing the middle-of-the-night walk of shame from my hookup's room when I spotted a familiar figure stumbling around outside by the pool.

"Amelia, can you help me?" Sunny slurred. "I don't feel so great, and I don't know where Ryan is."

She was walking toward me, reeling really, still feeling the effects of Roxy's roofies, poor thing. And that's when it happened. She tripped—I don't know if it was over a lounge chair or over her own two feet—and I heard a sickening thud. It must have been the sound of her hitting her head on the side of the pool, though I didn't know that at the time. Next thing I knew she was in the water, in the deep end, struggling and flailing, crying for help. It was a pathetic little cry, more like a whimper, really.

"Don't worry, I'm coming," I told her, looking around to see if anyone else was out and about. It was only us. The stars twinkled in the sky, and the palm fronds rustled in the gentle breeze.

What a wonderful spring break we'd had, all in all. I remember thinking that I should probably hurry, but another, stronger force told me no. My self-preservation button activated, and it wouldn't turn off. I had a reputation and a future to protect.

Because the fact is, unlike with Jamie, the thought to save her crossed my mind for only a split second. And then it was replaced by self-preservation. I mean, Jamie really is a good girl underneath all that drug addiction, she really is. Except of course she killed Brett in cold blood. So, I guess she isn't really better than me now, is she?

I'm afraid I would say I'm worse. I'm rotten through and through. That's why my husband's job in the Senate was a perfect setting for me. DC is full of liars and cheats and chameleons, almost all of them. They're out for themselves, they're familiar that way, and I'm proud to be in their ranks. I've found my people, so to speak.

That night, I did walk over to the pool, I did. The lights on under the water created strange shadows, but I could see Sunny's shape, her petite frame still struggling for air, for help. She brought her head up out of the water as I sat down by the side of the pool. She looked at me. I think she saw me, before her beautiful green eyes rolled back and her head went under again. It didn't take more than my hand on the top of her head to hold her underwater. She barely fought me at all. Perhaps it was a relief after the confusing, stumbling evening she'd had.

It only took a few minutes to silence Sunny for good. I know that sounds crass, and chilling, and a little bit evil, but it had to be done. It all worked out in the end, for everyone but Sunny. And we'll let Jamie believe it was mostly her fault Sunny died. It will be a good talking point for her in therapy, one of the many things an addict needs to work through. She seemed to need some sort of confessional, and now she's had it. And who knows, really? Maybe Sunny was still alive when Jamie found her. I mean, it's not like I fished her out of the pool to check for a heartbeat.

I killed two birds with one stone that night. Not only did I graduate without anyone knowing my family and I were destitute—there wasn't time or energy in the sorority to replace Sunny as treasurer—but I also hit the jackpot with Roxy. It was easy to blackmail her over the roofies after what happened to Sunny. I mean, it was almost my obligation. And sure, Dick, my poor husband, may he rest in peace, was wealthy—I wouldn't have married him otherwise—but it's always nice for a girl to have her own side hustle, as they say. Roxy was mine.

Roxy would have paid anything to keep Ryan in the dark, and she did. I'm going to need to replace that monthly allowance. I rely on that money, I really do. I mean, Dick's estate was fine, but I was expecting more. Another annoying thing about the man. He kept me on the tightest budget all through our marriage and continued the tradition after he died. And, no, I didn't kill him. That would be too cliché, right? The widow who killed her spouse to get what she wanted. No, he died of a heart attack, pure and simple. Now, if I had known Jamie's trick, I might have considered it. But I digress.

Jamie will be my new Theta Gam lifeline, my new side hustle. Guilt is such a wonderful tool. She'll pay, or I'll send her to prison. Oh, I know Beth made us pinky promise to stick together, made me promise not to blackmail Jamie, to keep her secret. But too bad. It's every woman for herself. Always has been.

51

AMELIA

I look up and enjoy the clear, blue sky. It's a shame everything is coated in sand and dust out here. It really was a beautiful place. What? Who is that? I blink and take off my sunglasses. And sit up. Goose bumps dot my skin.

It's a woman, and even after I blink a few more times, she's still there. She's on the far side of the pool, hurrying toward the main house. It's Sunny. But it can't be. As I watch, she stops and turns. She's wearing a maxi-length green sundress, large sunglasses, and a sparkling tennis necklace. It's her outfit, it's her look. It's her. Oh my God.

"Sunny?" I say in a whisper. I swallow as fear wells up in my throat. I stand and hold on to the back of the lounge chair to keep from falling. This can't be happening, but it is. This is what I get for what I did. Maybe this is what I deserve. Ghosts return for revenge. She's come for me.

She stops walking and turns and looks at me. I'm shaking all over. Will she suddenly charge me, float across the pool and grab me, hold me under the water until I drown? Impossible scenarios rush through my head. But instead of coming toward me, she turns away and hurries toward the house. Where is she going? What is she going to do to me?

I've never felt so startled and disoriented. Do I follow Sunny, ask her to forgive me, or do I simply pretend she isn't here, that she doesn't know everything? What would she do to me if I chased her? What can ghosts do to the person who murdered them?

I've decided I don't need that Bloody Mary after all. I start running as fast as I can in the opposite direction from where Sunny went amid the fallen branches and debris from the storm. I run inside the pool house where I've been staying. I look around at my clothes strewn everywhere, at Brett's suitcase, open, full of his things. My three suitcases are empty, but I don't have time to pack. I can replace stuff. I dart into the bathroom and grab my favorite face cream and my toothbrush. I see Brett's sitting on the counter and get a little pang of sadness, but there's no time for that. And there's no time to take anything else with me. I grab my purse, and my keys and my sunglasses.

I got the message loud and clear. Sunny doesn't need to warn me again. This is her house, and I better get out of here. I use the side path Brett and I discovered when we first arrived and find the ornamental wrought-iron gate. I push it open and hurry to the driveway. My red sports car is where I left it, and, thank God, it's undamaged.

My hand shakes as I unlock the door and hop behind the wheel. I am suddenly sober, more sober than I've been this entire weekend. Dead sober and terrified. I punch the gas, navigating around fallen palm fronds on the circular driveway. I check the rearview mirror as I reach the end of the circle and I'm about to lose sight of Gentry House.

She's there, standing on the driveway. Her hands are on her hips. She's watching me. What does she want? Oh my God. I push the gas pedal, urging my car to go faster. I swallow and lean forward. I want to get out of here so badly, I know I'm frantic. I'm in panic mode. I don't want to think about what she would do to me if she knew the truth. She likely knows the truth, right? She's dead. I killed her.

I glance up and look into the rearview mirror, and she's gone. I remind myself to concentrate on the road, knowing trees are down everywhere, but I don't see it in time. I'm going too fast. I slam on the brakes, but it's too late.

The last thing I hear is the sound of my own scream before everything goes black.

I've decided most people get what they deserve in life. But Sunny didn't deserve to die. I've learned everything I could about her, even reading old newspaper articles, so I could become her, for him. I like to help Ryan with his grief. It was unfair, and he's still hurting. So, I play along. It's the least I can do for the love of my life. Today, I'm simply wearing a green dress, like the ones Sunny loved, and a beautiful necklace Ryan gave me when we first started dating. Some people might think it's odd that our relationship is based on how much I resemble his dead ex-lover. But I don't mind. I have friends who are dating guys with much less in common. It's true. Ryan fell in love with me because I look like her, like she looked when she died. Hopefully, he doesn't expect me to stay this way forever. I mean, I'm not a ghost; I'm alive. Since we've been together, I've read, listened to Ryan's memories, examined all the photos of her he has kept all these years. I'm confident I look the part. But after all her old sorority sisters finally leave here, leave our home and go back to wherever they came from, hopefully Ryan will let me be me. Kat.

52

BETH

"What was that noise?" I ask Ryan.

"What?" he says. He's still pushing me against the window, pressing my shoulder against the cold glass, texting someone on his phone. Finally, the sound of crunching gravel gets his attention. He looks over my head out the window.

"Oh, that was good old Amelia departing rather suddenly. She didn't even say goodbye. And from what I could see as I watched her hurry to her car and drive off, she left her pile of pink baggage behind, all of it—oh, and she left Brett," Ryan says. When he laughs a chill runs down my spine. I used to like his laugh. I used to like him. I am fairly certain he's lost his mind. "She should have at least taken the body with her. I mean, she is the one who brought him here, and neither of them was invited. Rude, if you ask me."

It's official. He's no longer the Ryan I knew. "So, that means the roads are clear now?"

"Maybe. Who knows," Ryan says.

All I know is I'd rather take my chances out there in the desert than spend another minute in here with a madman. "Oh, great. We can leave too. I'll be on my way," I say. I'm nervous, sweaty. I try to wriggle out of his grip, but it's not working. "Let me go, please."

"You know, I'll always remember that night with you," he says. He leans in close to my face, too close. "Both because the sex was surprisingly good, and then, of course, the shame and regret because of Sunny. What if she had lived? What if she had found out about us? What would have happened? You tempted me. You were an untrue friend. It was all your fault that night, you bitch."

"We would have told her we were drunk, and we made a terrible mistake," I say, staring into his eyes. His eyes glisten with threats.

"Wrong answer. We never would have told her. She wouldn't have gotten over it, ever," he says.

"It doesn't matter anymore. Let me go," I say.

He shoves his phone into his pocket and grabs my other shoulder, spinning me around so I'm facing out the window. What, who is that? Standing on the driveway, her back to us, is a woman with long blond hair wearing a green dress. I shake my head and close my eyes. When I open them, she's still there. She's the woman on the postcard, the woman in the photos.

"Who is that?" I ask. My heart pounds in my chest. It can't be her. She's dead.

"My girlfriend. Sunny," Ryan says.

As if on cue, the woman in the green dress turns around. She looks up to the window and smiles.

I'm shaking all over. I don't know what this is, who she is, but I need to get out of here. I kick Ryan in the groin, bend my knees, drop to the ground fast, and dart away, running to the door.

"Stop, Beth, we're not finished here," he says, hobbling in pain trying to catch me.

I reach the door and pull on the handle at the same moment Ryan catches up to me. He grabs my hair with one hand and my waist with the other.

"I told you we aren't finished," he says in a growling voice.

"What do you want?" I ask. I feel his breath hot on my face.

"I want you to suffer. I want you to die alone," he says.

"Sure, OK, it looks like that's where I'm headed," I say. "Not going to be a problem."

"Promise me you won't tell her about that night," he says. "It will ruin everything we've built together. Oh, and don't tell Roxy about Sunny. She'll find out soon enough."

That's all? "No problem. I promise," I say.

He lets go of my hair and takes his arm away from my waist. "I always did like you, Beth. I always did, until you tricked me, seduced me, that night. You are the one. Not me. That's why I watched your girl, that's why I'm taking her away from you. Celeste will be a Gentry. You'll be all alone, like you deserve."

"Uh-huh," I say and grab my purse from the dresser, debating whether I should try to bring my suitcase with me too.

"Let me help you with your bag," Ryan says, grabbing my suitcase, as gallant as if the past few minutes never happened. It's unsettling how Ryan vacillates from livid to the perfect host at the drop of a hat. His shifting emotions are troubling.

I walk quickly down the hall and reach the front door, thrilled to be getting away from this place. I open the door.

"Mom, there you are," Celeste says. She and Zach are sitting on a bench, suitcases beside them. Despite what he thinks, Ryan will not take my girl from me. Ever.

"Here I am. Let's get going," I say. I look ahead down the path, but there is no sign of Ryan's *girlfriend*, thank God.

"Zach, are you leaving too?" Ryan says.

"Yeah, Dad, everyone is leaving. Mom already left with Jamie and Greer. She looked like she'd seen a ghost. I mean, there is a dead body in the living room, so there's that," Zach says. "Are you staying here?"

"Yes. This is my home," Ryan says. I don't have to look at him to know his eyes are darkening. "This is where I'm meant to be."

"What's wrong with you, Dad? You look weird," Zach says. Celeste takes his hand.

"Let's go," she says. She looks at me, and I nod.

"Yes, let's go," I say. "I can handle my own suitcase." I hope he'll let us all leave. I hope his ghostly girlfriend doesn't reappear.

"Safe travels," Ryan says and hands me the suitcase handle. He leans in close and whispers, "I'll be watching you, Beth. And Celeste too. As always. You will pay for what you did."

A chill runs down my spine. He has been spying on us this entire weekend, I'm certain of it now. And he's been watching me for years, too, waiting to exact his revenge. He blames me for the night we hooked up, when in reality he was the one who needed a place to sleep. Why didn't he go to the front desk and get another key? Because the Desert Sunrise wasn't like that, I know. The night staff was gone by eight p.m. But that doesn't excuse what he's done now. He had a plan to take Celeste from me, by introducing her to Zach. Oh my God. I hurry down the walkway tugging my suitcase, with Celeste and Zach close behind.

We reach my car, miraculously undamaged by the windstorm, toss our bags in the trunk, and hurry inside. We are all spooked, I realize.

Celeste is in the front seat next to me, and Zach is in back. I start the car and begin to drive away. I look in the rearview mirror and Sunny's there, with Ryan, standing on the driveway. Zach is looking out the back window and sees them too. They're holding hands under the palms in front of a Desert Sunrise. I mean, no, it's not her.

I need to get away from here.

53

BETH

Zach leans forward and hits the back of my seat.

"Who's that with my dad, Mrs. Harris?" he says.

"Not sure," I say, which isn't a lie. I glance at them in the mirror and get goose bumps.

"Does he have a girlfriend?" he says. "Tell me what you know, please."

"To be honest, Zach, I'm really not certain what's going on," I say. I'm so glad to be leaving them in the past. Both of them.

"Well, that's messed up," he says. "I was blaming my mom for everything, for being so, well, herself, and he has a girlfriend? He's been cheating on my mom, sneaking around? This sucks."

"Mom, stop!" Celeste yells, bracing herself against the front dashboard. "A crash!"

I slam on the brakes. Off to the side of the road, a car has smashed into a tree. I recognize the car and my heart sinks.

Even though I know the truth about Amelia that she is capable of many terrible things, I don't think she deserved this type of gruesome ending. The car is a mangled mess. I hop out of the car and run to the accident scene. The front section of the red sport car is smashed in, collapsed onto itself, Amelia pancaked in the middle of it all. I stifle a scream as Celeste and Zach join me.

"Another person dead?" Zach says. "Isn't that one of the houseguests? The redhead? Amelia?"

"Yes, it's her. Celeste, don't look," I say, turning away.

"Is she alive? We need to call for help," Celeste says, pulling out her phone. "Damn, there's still no service."

"There's nothing we can do for her," I say wearily. I've now seen death up close again, in Palm Springs again. I'm shaking all over. "Let's go. We'll drive until we get service. We can call for help then." I hustle them back to the car. My hands shake as I slip back behind the wheel.

"You OK to drive, Mom?" Celeste asks.

"Yes, I'm fine," I say, my senses all on high alert. My response has kicked in big-time, and my heart is racing. I check the rearview mirror, half expecting to see Ryan and his mystery woman behind us, watching us again. Thankfully, they aren't. I put the image of the horrific accident out of my head and try to tell myself to relax and breathe. But I know that will happen only once we've put enough distance between us and this horrible place.

We drive in silence for half an hour. I take it slow, careful to drive around downed branches and power lines. It takes us another half an hour to reach a place that has electricity, and our phones begin to work again. I know we need to send help to that godforsaken house, but I also know if I call from my phone, I'll always be linked to everything that happened this weekend. I suppose I will be anyway, but I can create some distance. I don't want to be the star witness to the disaster this weekend was. And I've promised Jamie discretion. I pull into a gas station.

"I'll pump the gas, Ms. Harris," Zach says, slipping out of the car.

"Beth," Celeste says before he gets out of the car. Zach ignores the correction, as usual. Once he's outside pumping, she says, "So annoying he won't call you by your name."

"It's OK. There are bigger issues, I think, honey. I'd be more concerned that he is a lot like his mom, and his dad. It's a problematic gene pool, either way. Have you seen any signs of a temper? Narcissism?" I ask. "Ryan seems to have anger issues these days."

"I don't know. What signs?" she asks. "He's only been great to me."

"Good question. You know, I had no idea who Ryan truly was, not until this weekend together," I say, facing my daughter. "I didn't realize he'd never gotten over Sunny's death, that he'd truly never moved on from that night, in many ways."

"But he did. He married Roxy. They had Zach," she says, her eyes damp with tears. "They seemed like the perfect family. They have it all, don't they? At least I thought so until yesterday."

"You never know what goes on behind closed doors," I say. "But you could, maybe, take your time getting married? It's probably a good idea after this weekend."

She nods, wiping a tear with her finger. "We live together, though. What if he…"

The car door opens. Zach's back. I smile at him and then at Celeste. I decide we will not be the ones to call the police. There is nothing that can be done for Brett or Amelia, or for Ryan. He's found his own weird version of happiness.

As I pull back out on the highway, I pat Celeste's leg. You'll always have me, my touch says. And maybe that's the point of this whole weekend. Maybe I had to find out everything I never wanted to know about what really happened the night Sunny died, to fully appreciate my life. My daughter's life. And I've been careless. Now that I know what Ryan has become, I'll be watching him too. I'll make sure he stays far away from me, and Celeste and the future she will create with Zach. And I know another thing for certain: I'm finished interacting with all of my sisters.

"When's your flight back to Chicago, Zach?" I ask.

"We leave early this afternoon, from LAX, Ms. Harris. I moved our flights up a day. We appreciate the lift," he says. "You're still flying back home with me today, right, Celeste?"

I look at my daughter. She takes a deep breath. She pivots in her seat to face him.

"I'm going to spend some time with my mom," she says. "The weekend was, well, something. I need time to process everything. I'll let my adviser at school know. I'm sure she'll be fine with it. I can take classes online from home."

"Sure, yeah, whatever. But are we good, you and me?" he asks.

"Yes, I love you. I need a little time, with my mom, I really do," she says. "I saw so much this weekend. I'm spinning."

"Well, I did too. I understand. And I'm still flying home to Chicago. I've got too much to do before our next big shindig," Zach says. "I mean, I think Mom will still want to host a big engagement party. I know she had the invitations printed and sent already."

"Nothing is going to get in the way of your mom throwing a party, you're right," I say. I feel sorry for Zach and Celeste. This is all so unsettling. I'm not sure what, if anything, to tell them both about Ryan. Except, maybe, to stay away from him.

I can't help but insert myself into the conversation. I'm right here, in the car. "Did your dad tell you to meet Celeste? Did he tell you who she was? Was this all arranged?"

Zach shrugs. "Sort of, I guess. Maybe my mom told him about Celeste? I really don't know. All I know is that he said she was gorgeous—he was right—and that she was the daughter of a special friend from college. I mean, he was looking out for me, like he always does."

I swallow and keep my eyes on the road. How did Ryan know Celeste was in Chicago? Roxy and I weren't in touch. How did he know she was gorgeous? Why would he put them together? A chill runs down my spine again. I suppose it's another link to Sunny, another tie to the past. It's not right.

"So your dad was on my daughter's social media, right?" I say carefully. It's the only way he could have gotten into her life, figured out where she went in Chicago, what her favorite things were.

"Sure, I guess he was," Zach says. "But he was right. We're meant to be together."

Celeste doesn't say anything, not right away. And then she says, in a quiet voice, "You never told me you knew who I was. You acted like it was a chance run-in when we met." She pauses, shakes her head. "To answer your question. You know what I'm afraid of? Your family. You haven't told me the truth about how we met. What else are you hiding or lying about?"

I focus on the road. She is right to be angry, but not at Zach. "Celeste, it's not Zach's fault."

Celeste takes a deep breath, turns, and reaches her hand out to Zach in the back seat. "You're right. I love you for you. It's not about your family."

I swallow. I shouldn't punish Zach for the sins of his father. It's not right.

"I love you, Celeste," Zach says. "We're meant to be."

"OK, you two. We need to get going if Zach's going to make his flight," I say. "Are you sure you want to come home with me, honey?"

Celeste looks at me and nods. "Can't wait. We both need some down time after this weekend."

Yes, we do. More than she even knows.

54

BETH

The lovebirds reluctantly parted ways at LAX as Zach hustled to make his flight.

We drive in silence for a while, and then Celeste says, "Was there ever anything between you and Ryan? I mean, he seemed to follow you around a lot, and he was always touching you, your shoulder, your arm. It was sort of creepy, to be honest."

No, there is absolutely nothing there. One big mistake. Some things are best left buried in the past if at all possible.

"When your best friend is dating somebody seriously, like Sunny and Ryan, it's natural to create a relationship with him," I say. "He was always around."

"I guess," she says. "But it seemed like more. I don't know. And then he had that young woman hidden away someplace. Where did she come from? The woman in the driveway when we left?"

I look over at Celeste. Where did she come from? A secret room in a secret house in the beautiful, now damaged compound that Ryan designed for his dead girlfriend and his new girlfriend, who looks just like her. It's much simpler than that.

"She came from Ryan's desire to bring Sunny back to life," I say. "Grieving the loss of a loved one, especially a romantic partner, is a deeply personal and complex experience."

"I hope I never have to find out about that," she says with a sigh.

"Oh, unfortunately, you will, honey. That's the saddest part of love. People cope in various ways. Ryan coped by sleeping with Roxy, falling into the arms of someone who put herself there for him, at every turn. Someone the opposite of Sunny, but it wasn't a fit; it never was a fit," I say. "Now he's finding companionship with a young woman who shares physical similarities with Sunny. There's no wrong or right way to handle grief."

I debate whether to tell Celeste that Ryan had been stalking us her entire life, stalking her, too, to ruin my life. To make sure I died alone, with Celeste sucked into their family and me left on the other side. He hated me, blamed me for everything that happened to Sunny, even though we both fell into each other's arms. He turned his own guilt into rage against me, incapable of blaming himself. I don't want to scare Celeste any further, and thankfully, she's out of the Gentrys' clutches for the time being.

"That had to freak you out, Mom. She looks like Sunny, exactly the way you described her to me, frozen in time. You've got to admit it was a little, I don't know, wrong," she says. "His wife and kid were there."

And Celeste hadn't even seen the mannequin fall from the sky.

"It was wrong, for sure. Unfortunately, I have more experience with disappointing men than you do. I hope you never do," I say. "Zach's a good guy. You'll have a wonderful life together." I smile at her and pat her shoulder. I pray he won't break my favorite daughter's heart, but fate may have other plans.

"I hope so, Mom. I really do," she says. She turns on the radio and flips to an all-news station. "I want to hear about the storm."

The voice over the radio says, "So far, there have been two confirmed deaths due to the severe windstorm experienced in Palm Springs. A forty-five-year-old woman smashed her car into a tree, and a fifty-year-old man drowned in a pool during the storm. Their names have not been released pending notification of relatives. Damage estimates continue to grow as many trees are down and the power has not been restored to the area."

Amelia and Brett. Once they discover who Amelia is, that she is on the cover of every society magazine in Southern California and Washington, DC, her story will get much more attention. I think about her kids, now orphans without a mom or a dad, and hope there is extended family to help them through all of this. Brett will be a footnote, I'm afraid, and likely won't be linked to her at all.

That's the thing about choices and fate. Roxy chose to drug

Sunny. Jamie chose not to help her when she was dying in the pool. Ryan chose to marry Roxy, who he didn't love, because of the son he knew he would. I chose the wrong man to marry, but I now have a beautiful daughter I wouldn't trade for the world. Brett chose to come along on the engagement weekend to torment Jamie, I suppose, and in a twist of fate, died because of her. And poor Amelia. She chose to crash this engagement weekend, I think, to torment us all, to wield her power. She had been blackmailing Roxy, and I know, I know, she would have blackmailed Jamie next, despite her promise not to do so.

Deep in my heart I have a feeling. A feeling that Sunny— the real Sunny—was there this weekend in the desert, watching over us in spirit. And deep in my heart, and my soul, I believe that Amelia got what she deserved. And maybe Sunny played a role in it. I know I sound as confused as Ryan, but I believe it. As soon as I reached the mangled car, I felt it. Amelia never confessed to anything, but the way she gloated when everyone began confessing, the way her eyes sparkled, the sinister red lipsticked, pursed-lip smile.

I wish Sunny could tell me herself, but in a sense, I think she did.

"Mom..." Celeste says, and I jump.

"Yes, sorry, lost in thought," I say. "What is it?"

"Thanks for coming to my engagement party," she says. "I don't know if I would have survived it without you."

"It was quite a weekend," I say. "You know I'm always going to be by your side. You're the favorite daughter. And next time you and Zach have something to celebrate, I'm hosting the party. Deal?"

"Deal," she says with a grin on her face. "It will be the best day ever."

"No yacht clubs," I say. "And no weekend-long, formal-attire situations."

"Nope," she says. "That's really not us."

"It's who I was afraid you were going to become, around the Gentrys," I say.

"Well, looks like you're stuck with me the way I am," she says. "I'm not going to change. Twizzlers?"

"Yes, please," I say and realize now that the shock of last night and this morning is wearing off, I'm starving. She hands me the candy, and I take a big bite. I feel my shoulders begin to relax as we chew in silence. We're almost home, home to my modest bungalow with peekaboo ocean views. I couldn't be more relieved. And as a bonus, I have somebody home with me. I know it won't last for long, and she'll likely head back to Chicago soon. But I'll enjoy every bonus minute with her.

Sunny will remain a sparkling memory, my long-lost best friend, but Celeste, she's everything. She and Zach have a wonderful future together, and I know I'll be an important part of it.

"I'm so happy you're coming home for a bit," I say. "Another Twizzlers, please?"

Celeste's laugh fills the car. "This is the last one. Enjoy!"

It's the end of a lot of things, I'm afraid. I know it's my job as a mom to resist the urge to beg her to choose me, not him.

That's not love; that's fear. The sun glints off the hood of my candy-apple-red Mustang. The Twizzlers is sweet and sour at the same time.

In the rearview mirror, the past is farther away by the mile.

ACKNOWLEDGMENTS

A profound thank you to my literary manager, Liza Fleissig of Liza Royce Associates, for her enthusiastic belief in me and my books. Working with you has been a game changer in so many ways.

Thank you to Diane DiBiase, my editor, for loving this story and making it better and to "real" Beth Deveny for her insights about pretend Beth and the other characters in *We Were Never Friends*. To the team at Sourcebooks and Poisoned Pen Press: I'm so happy to be working with you.

As always, my husband and my four kids—plus two added spouses—are forever in my heart and my biggest fans. Thank you Harley, Trace, Annika, Avery, Paul, Shea, and Dylan. My friends mean the world to me, and my college friends and sorority sisters are no exception. They are not the inspiration for this story.

I created the Killer Author Club for readers like you who enjoy mystery and suspense novels. With my cofounders, Kimberly Belle and Heather Gudenkauf, we host a biweekly live show and a podcast where we talk about killing—of the fictional kind, of course. Join us at killerauthorclub.com.

Special thanks to the bookstores and bookstagrammers, the bloggers and author community, and to you, the reader. I couldn't do the job of my dreams without you. Thank you from the bottom of my heart. Please reach out via social media and, if you'd like, sign up for my newsletter. I'd love to stay in touch!

ABOUT THE AUTHOR

Photo by Candice Dartez

Kaira Rouda is an award-winning, *USA Today*, Amazon Charts, and international bestselling author of contemporary fiction that explores what goes on beneath the surface of seemingly perfect lives. Her novels of domestic suspense include *The Widow*, *Somebody's Home*, *The Next Wife*, *The Favorite Daughter*, *Best Day Ever*, *All the Difference*, *Beneath the Surface*—optioned for a feature film—*Under the Palms*, *The Next Mrs. Strom*, *What the Nanny Saw*, and *Jill Is Not Happy*. To date, Kaira's work has been translated into more than a dozen languages. Three of her novels have been named Amazon Editors' Picks for Best Mystery, Thriller & Suspense. *The Next Wife* was named

Suspense Magazine's Best Book of 2021 and won a 2022 Silver Falchion for Best Suspense Novel and a 2022 Silver Falchion first runner-up for Best Book of the Year. *Beneath the Surface* won a Zibby's Media Award for Best Beach Read. *Jill Is Not Happy*, an instant *USA Today bestseller*, was named most anticipated book of 2025 by Zibby Media, CrimeReads, and *Crimespree Magazine*. Kaira is a founding member of the Killer Author Club, a bimonthly live show supporting authors. She is a member of Sisters in Crime, Mystery Writers of America, the Women's Fiction Writers Association, and the International Thriller Writers Association. She served as a committee chair for the Edgar Awards 2024 and frequently appears on panels at conferences across the country.

kairarouda.com

TikTok: @KairaRoudaBooks

Facebook: KairaRoudaBooks

Instagram: @KairaRouda

X: @KairaRouda